Withdrawn

BELOW

BELOW

MEG MCKINLAY

CANDLEWICK PRESS

Copyright © 2011 by Meg McKinlay

First U.S. edition 2013

Library of Congress Catalog Card Number 2012943652

ISBN 978-0-7636-6126-7

13 14 15 16 17 18 BVG 10 9 8 7 6 5 4 3 2 1

Printed in Berryville, VA, U.S.A.

This book was typeset in Minion.

Candlewick Press
99 Dover Street
Somerville, Massachusetts 02144

visit us at www.candlewick.com

For Alison, always interfrastical

The day that I was born, they drowned my town.

The mayor flipped the lever, and everybody cheered. There were streamers and balloons and a really lame brass band. The people of Old Lower Grange ate sausages and potato salad while they watched their lives sink beneath a wall of water.

I didn't see the town take its last gulping breath. No one in my family did.

That was my fault, of course. There was no way around it.

I was early. That was the thing. I was eight weeks early, and no one was expecting to see me that day.

Mom and Dad were going about their business, trying to decide whether it was morbid or festive to go and watch their old lives disappear under two hundred feet of water, when all of a sudden I was coming.

Mom yelled for Dad, and he left the plate he was making half-done on the table, where it would later crack down the center.

Years later they presented it to me on my birthday as a keepsake, the way other kids get their booties bronzed or their tiny handprints preserved in plaster.

Here, they said, *have this broken plate as a symbol of your birth. It would have been better, but you kind of got in the way.*

Okay, they didn't actually say that, but I knew it was what they were thinking.

Because of me, while everyone else was gathering at the dam, we were busy racing in the other direction. We were speeding through New Lower Grange, which had been thrown up just four miles east of the lever-flipping festivities — *hey, presto!* — as if someone had snapped open a page in a pop-up book. We were zipping past the instant lawns and the empty swimming pool and the hollow shells of buildings, out onto the highway, and then all the way over to Lenton, the closest town with anything resembling a hospital, for the occasion of my inconvenient birth.

By the time Mom and Dad brought me home, things were different. There was electricity in the supermarket and water in the pool. Below the ground's hard surface, lawns were sending down their tiny, invisible roots.

It was almost like a real town.

If she didn't look closely, my sister, Hannah, could pretend this was the street where she fell off her bike when she was six; my brother, Elijah, could tell himself the ridges in the twisty gum tree out front were from the tire swing he used to ride to the moon and back.

But there was no history here, not really.

When Mom and Dad laughed about the time Elijah threw a wad of mashed potatoes at Hannah, they all turned and stared at the back wall of the kitchen, then looked away again. There was supposed to be a stain on the wallpaper there, a fat circle of damp that had never quite come off.

But all those stories were dead and drowned. The mashed potatoes and the green-and-orange 1960s wallpaper had been replaced by easy-clean tiles with a trendy mosaic border. Our old lives were two hundred feet underwater at the bottom of a lake, and no one could bring themselves to care anymore.

No one except me.

When I was little, I used to dream about our house all the way down there in the mud. I pored over the photo albums lining the bookshelves in the hall and wondered what it all looked like now — the twisty old gum tree, the hairpin bend, the tree house out back that would have been mine.

When I first heard the story of Atlantis, I caught my breath. I took a lump of Dad's clay and made a model of a mermaid, only with short hair, like mine. In kindergarten, I drew pictures of us underwater. I drew all of us standing out in front of the house, holding hands under a bright sun, and Mrs. Morganstern gave me a gold star for excellence. Then I took a thick crayon and drowned us all in blue.

I never lived in Old Lower Grange, but I felt like I had. Like I should have. Like those two things were sort of the same.

And even though you couldn't see the damp patches on the walls anymore, I knew they were under there somewhere.

You'd think that when you sink something under five thousand swimming pools' worth of water, it'd be drowned and gone. You'd think it would be done with. But somewhere inside me, I knew — you can't just drown a town and call it over. Eventually, things have a way of floating to the surface.

One

It was the seven-Band-Aid swim that finally sank me.

I could have handled four, five, even six. Six had been my record until then.

It wasn't a record I'd wanted to break.

I cruised the last few feet in a slow breaststroke, keeping my head above water like a grandma, all the better not to see disgusting floating Band-Aids. I reached for the wall, slapping the tiles with both hands the way I'd learned in swimming classes.

"Exactly level," our PE teacher always said, leaning over us with a stopwatch like we were in the Olympics or something. "Or — *bam!* — disqualified!"

No one was really sure why he was teaching us this stuff. Most of us hadn't quite mastered the frog kick yet. Max Cartwright still swallowed water when he opened his mouth to breathe.

When we asked Mr. Henshall why it mattered, he shook his head. It was just one of those rules. Don't question — just do it. You could blitz the field, finishing half a lap ahead of second place, but if your hands weren't level on the wall or you got out before the whistle blew, it was all over.

I don't know why I kept doing it. I couldn't help myself, even when I wasn't racing, even when I was just doing my *six laps a day without fail, Cassie, okay?*

Six laps, every day over summer, up and down in my faded blue Speedo swimsuit while everyone else hung out on the grass in their stripy bikinis or dived and splashed and did cannonballs around me.

That's what the doctor said. Not the part about bathing suits and cannonballs. I don't think she really thought it through that far. She just said six laps. That it would be good for me — for my lungs, which weren't ready to be born when I was and had never quite caught up.

The doctor said it, so Mom said it, too.

When you feel like you can't breathe, that's when you dig in, Cassie. That's when it's doing you good.

My own theory was that when I felt like I couldn't breathe, I should probably stop and take it easy for a while. Luckily, Mom didn't come to the pool with me anymore; she just gave advice from a distance, then went back to grading papers.

I reached behind to squeeze water from my hair and took a deep, ragged breath. Something caught in my throat, and I coughed once, then twice, then again and again in short staccato barks.

I clamped my mouth shut and felt the coughs detonate inside, puffing out my cheeks like tiny explosions. I hooked my fingers over the edge of the pool and hunched in toward the side, hoping no one would notice.

Yeah, this was doing me good.

Voices yelled and feet slapped across the concrete. I lifted my head to peer over the edge. Liam Price was stumbling over himself, slipping on the wet tiles, falling toward me.

I pushed backward and down. I felt him land

in the water above, then plunge down, one knee clipping the edge of my shoulder.

For a few seconds, we were tangled underwater, a mess of arms and legs and frantic bubbles.

When I broke the surface, there were faces leaning over the edge of the pool.

Amber and Emily. Laughing.

"Sorry," Liam said. "They pushed me."

"What are you going to do about it?" Emily teased.

"This." Liam's hand sliced through the water, sending up a shower of spray.

"Hey!" Amber jumped back. She was grinning. They were just messing around, the way kids do — at least kids who haven't spent half their lives in the hospital or doing laps or being told by their mothers to take a break and not get overexcited, not to push themselves too hard. Unless, of course, you were doing your six, and it was time to *dig in*.

Amber patted at the damp patches spreading across her hot-pink bikini.

"Oh, well, I guess I'm wet now."

She took a step forward and dived in, arcing over my head into the water behind me. I turned to watch, the way I always did when Amber swam, when she cruised down the pool with a stroke that cut through the water like it wasn't there, a stroke that was smooth and fast and kind of *accidental,* as if she wasn't even trying.

It wasn't fair that someone who didn't care at all could swim like that.

I looked back at Liam. Then again, lots of things weren't fair when you thought about it.

As I turned, he headed past me toward the ladder and hauled himself out, his board shorts flapping around him.

They were too long, those shorts. Too long to be cool, too long to be comfortable. Too long to swim in without them sucking in and sticking to his legs. He was always pulling at them, peeling the material off his wet skin with one hand, holding them up at the waist with the other.

I heard Emily whispering about it in class one day. "His mother buys them a size too big. So they won't show."

I didn't know if that was true, but the shorts did the job, anyway. You couldn't see Liam's scars.

Everyone knew they were under there, though, even if he kept them covered. Even if he had long ago found a way of walking, a jerky kind of rhythm that smoothed out his limp so it was almost invisible. It didn't matter what any of us saw or didn't see. Because what happened to Liam's family was a story the whole town knew and couldn't forget if it tried.

Liam took a long step out of the pool, skipping the top rung of the ladder. As he left the water behind, he gathered the waistband of his shorts around him, pulling the drawstring in tightly. He did this seamlessly, like he wasn't even thinking about it, like this task — of keeping his too-large shorts up, of hiding his scars — was as natural to him as breathing.

He shot a glance behind him as he went, back at me. To see if I was watching, maybe? To see if I cared?

I wasn't. I didn't.

I was watching the water he'd pulled himself out of, the way it surged and pooled and settled back into itself.

I was watching the Band-Aid floating in his wake, coming toward me across the surface like a homing pigeon.

Two

When I got home, Dad had a finger in someone's eye and another in their ear.

I dropped my bag on the floor of the studio. "So, who is it this time?"

"Guess."

I stared at the clay shape in front of him and shook my head. I never got it right. Then Dad got all offended, said it was a shame I couldn't share his artistic vision and started jabbing disturbingly at the face with his sharp little tools.

The problem was, there didn't seem to be anyone who shared Dad's artistic vision, including the tourists he stopped on Main Street because they had such interesting heads.

Seven?

I grandma-stroked my way to the ladder and hung off it for a minute, stretching my arms until they tingled. Then I hauled myself out, not bothering to look back.

I wouldn't be coming here tomorrow. I had a better idea, one that had been sitting quietly in the back of my mind for I wasn't sure how long. Maybe always.

I would still do my six laps or something like it. Up at the lake, it would be harder to measure, but it would be better in so many ways.

It would be still and peaceful.

It would be Band-Aid-free.

It would be other things, too, but I wasn't going to think about that now.

I wasn't going to think about the empty streets and the broken buildings, the way they had turned themselves over to fish and weeds and who knows what else. It didn't matter what was down there below me in the quiet dark. Everyone knew that swimming was about staying on the surface.

When Dad presented them with their clay head, which always managed to look both like them but not — as if they were slightly out of focus or something — they nodded thoughtfully. They took a step back, sometimes two, and said things like *Oh, how interesting!* and *Well, you've certainly put a lot of work into it!* and *What's that lumpy bit on the side there?* Then they checked their watches and muttered something about *Not much space in the car* and *Wouldn't last two minutes around the kids* and *No, no, you keep it* and *Oh, please, I insist.*

Usually, the heads ended up in our backyard, their weird angles and smashed features staring out from bushes and long grass and the forks of gum trees, like some kind of creepy zombie museum.

I studied the misshapen lump of clay. Was it even a head yet? Maybe that bit in the middle was a nose? On the other hand, it could just be a blob Dad had left there by accident.

I grinned and shook my head.

Dad sat back on his stool and sighed. "I probably shouldn't be doing this now, anyway." He motioned at the mess of half-finished work piled around us, all the pots and plates and other touristy knickknacks he was supposed to be getting ready for the summer tourist season.

He had to finish the firing and the glazing. Then he had to get it all into town, packing it carefully so it wouldn't shatter on the way or develop hairline cracks that would give the tourists who wandered into Country Crafts Gift Shop a reason to bargain down the price.

Dad clapped his clay-caked hands together and stood up slowly from his stool, wincing as his knees clicked in protest. "Nearly dinnertime. I'd better wash up."

"Yeah." I bent down to unzip my bag. My damp towel was balled up in there. I needed to hang it up before Mom came along to issue her gentle reminder.

Dad glanced at me. "How was your swim?"

"Okay." I shrugged. "Seven."

"*Seven?*" He let out a low whistle. "Yuck."

"Tell me about it." I followed him out the door and down the hall.

In the kitchen, Mom was stirring a thick soup on the stove. "Did you do your six?"

I slid into my chair. "Yep."

"Okay?"

"Yep."

She turned. "Hang your towel?"

"Yep."

"Good." She smiled.

"Hey, Cass. Check this out." Hannah was at the table, her work satchel hanging over the back of the chair.

Her laptop sat open in front of her, precariously balanced on a pile of papers.

She reached underneath it and pulled the top sheet from the pile. It was a newspaper article — faded and brittle-looking, as if it might flake into tiny pieces at any moment.

I glanced down at the date. It was old. Twelve years old, in fact.

There was a headline — "Welcome to New Lower Grange!" — and a grainy black-and-white photo: two people holding a bundle of something.

Two familiar people. Mom with a tired smile, Dad with a deer-in-the-headlights expression.

A bundle of me.

15

Hannah grinned. "I was just telling Mom." She made air quotes with her fingers. "'First baby born in New Lower Grange.' You're going to be in it, Cass."

I stared at her. "Me?"

I didn't need to look at Hannah's laptop to know what she was working on. It was the centenary book. Everyone in town knew about it. In the first place, it was that kind of town — so small everyone couldn't help but know everyone else's business. In the second place, this was the biggest news to hit New Lower Grange in as long as I could remember. The centenary of the town. Both towns, really.

Twelve years here, our teacher Mrs. Barber said, and eighty-eight . . . *you know*. She waved a hand toward the window in the general direction of the lake.

They had realized kind of at the last minute — that twelve plus eighty-eight equals a hundred. That it equals a centenary and another opportunity for a bunch of ceremonial sausages and a really lame brass band. That they had only a few short months to get ready.

A few weeks ago, Mrs. Barber rushed into class

with a panicked expression. She cleared her desk and wiped down the board. She told us to forget about Antarctica and penguins and global warming and the soap-making business we had been looking forward to all year, because Lower Grange was celebrating one hundred years of history, and we all had to do our part. We had to do handprints and mosaics. And eight-hundred-word essays entitled "My Lower Grange" with a clearly defined beginning, middle, and end, which would be sealed into a time capsule and dug deep into the ground for future generations to laugh at.

"See?" Hannah interrupted my thoughts. "It's going to be a kind of before-and-after. The growth of our town and all that. You'll be here." She scrolled with the mouse and pointed to a double-page spread that appeared on the screen.

"Cassie," she had written, in short, hurried text. "First baby, etc."

The middle. That's where I'd be, drawing the line between before and after.

"There's a lot of work to do." Hannah sighed. "But Howard says it's coming along nicely."

I nodded. Howard was Howard Finkle, the mayor of Lower Grange for the last seventeen years and counting, the man who'd flipped the lever to drown the old place. Hannah worked for him down at the town hall, putting together brochures telling tourists about the "vibrant arts culture" and the "laid-back country lifestyle," and writing press releases about all the fantastic things the town council was doing for our community.

Elijah always teased Hannah about her job. Spin, he called it. Finkle-spin. Making the town council look good. Making the mayor look good.

Finkle's face was on all of Hannah's papers, smiling out from the corner as if he was watching over the town and everything that went on here. He was that kind of guy — always smiling and joking and popping up anywhere, anytime, especially if there was the chance of a party or a ceremonial sausage or two. When we did Jump Rope for Heart at school, he came along and turned the rope for us. When we had Sports Day, he ran in the parents' race, even though his kids had grown up and moved away years ago. It was funny to see him hurl himself down the track, panting, his tie flapping loosely around his neck like a flag gone mad in the wind.

I stared down at my grainy photo.

It wasn't like I hadn't seen it before. In fact, I had a copy of that exact photo stuffed into a box under my bed — the box Mom thought was tucked away, *out of sight, out of mind,* in the shed.

"Moira and Andrew Romano," the caption read, "welcome Baby Romano. First New Lower Grange Baby! Sister to Hannah and Elijah."

Baby Romano. I rolled my eyes. That was my name back then. Mom and Dad said it was because I was so early, that they hadn't had time to settle on anything, that they were giving it long and careful thought, trying to find the exact right one.

But I knew the truth. I had seen Hannah's photo album — bright pink and tied in ribbon, full of elaborately displayed cards and photos and the letter Mom had written to *My dear Hannah* on fancy notepaper months before she was even born, her curly name just sitting there, waiting for her to arrive.

I'd seen Elijah's as well — shiny and blue and bursting with school photos and colorful slips of paper where Mom had jotted down notes about his favorite stewed vegetables and his sleep times and random cute things he had said when he was two.

And a birth notice carefully pressed onto the opening page. "Brother to Hannah," it read. "A perfect pair — the Romano family is now complete!"

My own so-called album was stuffed underneath them. It was one of those plastic display folders Mom used in her classroom, with a handful of school photos and a couple of old crayon drawings crammed in the front.

They were going to make me a proper album one day, she said. When they had time. When they could get their heads around the whole thing, the whole thing that was me.

Because it wasn't just that I was early. I was unexpected, too. I was accidental.

By the time I came along, Mom and Dad were done having kids. Hannah was twelve, and Elijah was ten. Mom had gone back to teaching history at the junior high school, and Dad was expanding his pottery hobby into a business.

When I was born, they smiled tired smiles in the

newspaper and named me *Rachael, no, Isobel, no, Sarah, no, Cassandra and maybe Cassie for short, yes, okay — well, I guess that's that, then.*

Later they said things like *lovely surprise* and *happy accident* and *Oh, we just kept on trying until we finally got it right.*

But I knew.

That I was extra. I was tacked on the end.

That our real family happened before, that it was over now, underwater.

Mom leaned over my shoulder. "What a photo. I look exhausted!" She pressed one hand to her temple and rubbed an imaginary spot. "No wonder, I suppose. All those weeks in the hospital. That horrible incubator. Thank goodness that's all behind us!"

I nodded. Yeah. All I had to deal with now was the endless struggle to breathe. The endless swimming. The endless Band-Aids.

"Hey!" Dad pushed his way through the door. "We going to eat or what? I'm starving."

Mom waved the ladle at him, sending tiny specks of soup flying through the air. "Minestrone."

"Great." Dad rubbed his hands together.

Mom smiled. "How's it all going?"

"Good." Dad threw a look at me. It was a look I knew, one that said, *Don't tell her about the head.*

I wouldn't have, anyway. People need secrets, I figure. People need things that are only for them.

In a quiet corner of my mind, the lake spread out, silent and still.

Three

After dinner, in my room, I pulled the box out from under the bed, shuffling it slowly across the carpet. I eased the lid off and stared down at the pile.

It had been a while since I'd looked at all of this — the newspaper clippings, the photographs, the crooked hand-drawn maps.

Even my old Atlantis drawings were down at the bottom somewhere, buried under the layers.

I guess that was fitting, if you thought about it in a certain way.

I reached down into the pile. This had all been organized once. It had been sorted by date and place and category.

There had been a point to it back then.

It had kept me busy. It had kept me sitting happily in a corner of Mom's history classes for a whole week one year when my school vacation didn't overlap with hers.

She was teaching her seventh-graders about the flooding of Old Lower Grange — about the discussion and debate, the town meetings and the protests. She said history was important, that you couldn't understand the present without thinking about the past. She stood at the front of the room and wrote on the whiteboard: *How can you know where you are if you don't know where you've been?*

I was seven then. I sat in the corner and listened. I watched while Mom's students nodded and frowned and did what she told them. They had mock debates, making arguments *for* and *against*. They compared maps of the old town and the new one, writing essays about what was the same and what was different, what had been gained, what had been lost.

I walked around the classroom. I looked over their shoulders and remembered my drawings of Atlantis, of our drowned family, faces obscured behind a thick wall of blue.

This was my town, I thought. This was the place

where my family grew. The place I came eight weeks early to see and missed by less than a day.

I collected photocopied clippings that the big kids had finished with. I cut up leftover photos and made scenes to fit them into. I drew maps and diagrams. I wrote a story about the day of the flooding, based on eyewitness accounts.

At first, Mom smiled. She called me *her little historian*. She held my work up in front of her classes and said they could all take a page from my book. She said if I was one of her students, she'd be giving me an A.

Weeks later, when I was still working on my maps, redrawing them over and over to add new details, when I had broken a month's worth of Dad's plates hunting through the old newspapers he had wrapped them in, when I couldn't sleep at night for dreaming about our house being engulfed by layers of silt and mud, Mom said it was time to stop.

She said what I had done was great, but now it was getting unhealthy, that I needed to think about other things, to live in the present.

Enough, she said, *was enough.*

Together, we packed it away into a box — *out of sight, out of mind.* I stopped drawing maps and poring over photos. But I kept dreaming — about the town, about Atlantis. I couldn't stop myself from doing that, even if I had wanted to.

And when I walked through the town, I felt the old one behind it. I could stand on Main Street and see Tucker's Supermarket the way it used to be — the wild orange and yellow rather than the new, tasteful blue. I could pause at the entrance to the pool and see the old timber mill, smell the earthy warmth of freshly cut wood, hear the whine of the saws that had stopped working before I was born. On the edge of town, I had to stop myself from looking up to find the old fire lookout, the tree with its circular staircase of pegs disappearing into clusters of leaves.

When I closed my eyes, Old Lower Grange was there, like that echo of light that sits inside your eyelids, etching shapes into quiet, secret spaces.

And every now and then, I pulled the box out from under my bed. Every now and then, I snipped something from the paper and added it to the pile, just because it seemed important not to let things go.

I didn't tell Mom. I wasn't sure she would consider it healthy. But whatever it was, I wanted to keep it.

I reached into the box and riffled through some old newspaper articles. They were mostly photocopies Mom had made for her class, the paper shiny and smooth in a way that seemed at odds with the stories they told. But there were a few that weren't copies. They were older, brown and brittle with age and bearing traces of the clay they'd once been packed around and between.

When I came to one of these, I stopped. It was an article about the lake, almost as old as I was. There was a photograph of the wide, calm surface. Trees and bushy scrub hugged the water's edge, and you could see the dam wall in the distance. A family was picnicking on the bank up at the Point. A couple of kids were messing around in a canoe.

And off to the right, a shadow. Something that could have been a glitch on the film or the blurred border of the photo.

It wasn't either of those things. I knew that because I'd been there with Dad in a canoe once, all the way out in the middle, where the sounds of people yelling and calling on the shore faded so far into the background, they sounded like the edges of a dream.

I remember Dad stopping the canoe. He brought it around in a flurry of back-paddling into an urgent, swooping arc, as if there was an invisible line there in the water, as if crossing it would mean something to someone.

It was just a metal pole. Just a sign, bobbing lazily out there on a floating buoy.

NO SWIMMING BEYOND THIS POINT, it said.

"We're not swimming," I pointed out, but Dad shook his head.

"It doesn't just mean swimming," he said. "It means no recreation area. Off-limits."

"But why?"

He shook his head again. There was no point asking. It was just one of those rules.

He back-paddled. We headed for shore. And we didn't go out that far again.

It was silly, anyway, according to Dad. It was reckless. What if something had happened when we were out there, such a long way from anywhere and anyone?

I ran a finger along the shadow on the photo.

I probably wouldn't see the pole tomorrow, not from where I planned to be. I wasn't going to take the road all the way around to the Point, where everyone else swam. Even though that would be quieter than the pool, there could still be other people there — yelling and splashing and churning up the surface with Jet Skis. And it was too far on a bike. To get there, you needed a car, a plan, a family outing.

Tomorrow I'd be taking a shortcut. It had been years since I'd been that way, and I'd never done it alone. The path had been tricky enough to spot back then. Now it would probably be completely invisible.

But I wasn't worried about that.

I was sure I could remember.

Four

On the way, the signs were so weathered I could hardly read them. Rust had eaten tiny holes in the metal, so it looked like someone had shot them over and over with a pellet gun.

That didn't matter. I knew what they said.

NO ENTRY. TRESPASSERS PROSECUTED.

That one was on the barrier just off the main road, the barrier I could easily lift my bike up and over onto the overgrown track that led up the hill.

AUTHORIZED PERSONS ONLY. ACCESS PROHIBITED.

That one was right up the top, hanging loosely from the padlocked gate of the wire-mesh fence.

The gate sat at the end of an old dirt road that wound its way around and around the hill, occasionally crossing the steep path I had taken. I supposed authorized persons needed to come up here sometimes, although I wasn't sure what for. Maybe just to check if there were any trespassers who needed prosecuting. The dirt road was completely overgrown, too. Elijah and I had never seen anyone up here, and it didn't look like that had changed.

I pushed my bike through the undergrowth, hunting for the break in the fence, the panel of loose wire you could peel back and slip quietly inside. Elijah and I found it together years ago, by accident. We were walking around the lake from the swimming area, talking and skipping stones and letting our feet carry us along the shoreline. At some point, we looked back at the tiny figures swimming and jumping and picnicking on the grass and realized that without meaning to, we had come almost halfway around. Halfway from the Point, halfway to . . . where? And we realized then that there *was* a somewhere else, that you could just keep going through the trees and the scrub and past the invisible line of the NO SWIMMING pole and find yourself somewhere that might even be worth going to.

31

That's how we found this place, on the other side of where we were supposed to be, a secret shore all our own.

I was worried about being there at first, worried that we would get in trouble. I pointed out that we had crossed the invisible line.

But Elijah just shrugged and said, "So what?" Even when we found the fence through the trees, the concealed path leading down the hill, the signs that yelled at you to stay away.

"People shouldn't worry about fences and signs," he said. If you let a see-through fence stop you, you mustn't have cared much in the first place.

After that day, whenever he jumped on his bike, his towel stuffed in his backpack, and asked if I wanted to come "for a ride" with him, I always said yes.

It was nicer around this side. It was still and quiet. You didn't have to watch out for Jet Skis or speedboats. There was no one to tell you to wait thirty minutes before going in the water because you had eaten a single slice of apple.

But there was something else, too.

There was Old Lower Grange.

The swimming area was over the outskirts of the old town, over paddocks and bush and the occasional shed. But here you were closer to the town itself, to the buildings and the roads and the houses where people had lived, where they had gotten married and pushed children on swings and tormented each other with gobs of flying mashed potatoes.

It was all out there somewhere. I watched the way the ground sloped down to the water's edge and beyond, and thought about it all there, underwater.

We swam along the shoreline, Elijah setting the pace, his long, measured strokes between me and the deep.

We floated on our backs, looking up at the cloudless sky, and I couldn't shake the feeling that there were things down below, things I shouldn't turn my back on.

Sometimes we stood in the shallows, skipping stones out across the water, seeing how many skips we could get until they sank out of sight. Then we'd guess where they'd landed — the town square, the school, our very own drowned tree house?

Sometimes we found things that might have washed up from the old town — a plank of wood from a fence, an old cookie tin, the wheel from a bike — but there was no way to be sure. For all we knew, they could have just been bits of junk that people had dumped there later.

Once I saw a road — the weathered edge of a sheet of dark stones, tightly packed, leading down and away.

The maps I had drawn in Mom's class clicked into place inside my head. We were on the west side of the lake and on high ground, so it could be the Old Lenton Road, where it ran up and away into the hills. That would make the school over there and the supermarket over there and our place would be . . .

I turned and scanned the water, the old streets laying themselves out like a jigsaw puzzle before my eyes, every piece perfectly formed to fit only and exactly in one rightful place.

It made me feel strange, shivery. I couldn't help imagining myself following it, putting one foot in front of the other, all the way down into the dark underwater town.

But Elijah shook his head. "That's not a road," he said. "See?"

He scrambled down the bank and kicked at the

stones. They came away easily under his shoe, and I saw that they weren't black, not tightly packed, but loose and irregular, a patchwork of colors. Just a random assortment of stones masquerading as a way to somewhere.

"But there could be roads," I said.

Elijah shrugged. "I guess."

"We could find one," I said. Now that the idea was in my head, it was difficult to shake. "We could follow it."

Elijah laughed. "It's not Atlantis, you know."

I knew he wasn't laughing *at* me, though. He had one of my old drawings stuck to the inside of his closet where he thought I couldn't see it.

"Anyway," he said, "it wouldn't work. You'd just keep bobbing to the surface."

He was right. But I didn't want him to be. I wanted to believe that somehow my feet would stay suctioned to the ground, that if I found a road, it would lead me down.

Maybe, I thought, I could make myself heavy. I could put stones in my pockets and bundle them up in my T-shirt.

"You want to weigh yourself down with stones and walk into a lake in the middle of the bush?" This time Elijah *was* laughing at me. "Idiot. This is why Mom doesn't let you swim on your own."

That night, I dreamed about Old Lower Grange. I saw the streetlights hung with lake weed, dark fists of mud, punched into the holes in the road. Crabs and crayfish made their homes in the hollowed-out buildings, and fish cruised the streets, pausing at intersections to politely wave each other through with their fins. I couldn't help wondering what kind of life was going on down there without us.

I never walked into town, though.

We never found a road. I kept half an eye out for sheets of stones but never saw anything. Then the rain came and the water level crept up, and even the pile of stones I kept going back to have a closer look at disappeared under the surface.

I stopped going up to the lake.

Elijah moved to the city for college, and Hannah started working for the town council. And she wasn't the kind of person who would walk past signs and slip through a hole in the fence. She was more likely to redo the lettering and tighten the wire.

Soon after, Mom started letting me go to the pool on my own. As long as I was sensible, she said. I was old enough now, and the pool was safe. It was much better than a lake. It had lifeguards and clear water. There were no shifting depths or hidden dangers, unless you counted people randomly jumping on you or slamming you with tennis balls. And it was clean as well, unless you counted the Band-Aids.

So I didn't go back to the lake. Not to look. Not to float or skip stones or wonder about fish.

Not until today.

Five

Dry sticks crackled underfoot as I came out of the trees into the open near the lake's edge. The water stretched out in front of me, a shifting expanse of color, sparkling in the light.

In spite of myself, I glanced along the shoreline toward where I'd seen the stones.

The water would be low; I knew that. It had been a dry year. A dry couple of years.

But I wasn't going to go over there — not this time.

Things were different now. I was older, for one thing, and smarter. I was only here to swim — to do my six without Band-Aids and stealth attacks. I wasn't about to fill my pockets full of stones and head off down a drowned road to who knows where.

I peeled my shirt off over my head and hung it on a low branch. Shoes, socks, shorts. I shook my orange towel out like a bird showing off its bright feathers and laid it down on the bank.

Then I took a deep breath, a handful of steps, and kicked off, out and away from the shore.

The water was cold and warm and clear and dark. It was so many things all at once.

Dragonflies hung in the air nearby, ghosting their shadows on the water around me. Tiny stick insects skimmed their way across the surface, following their own invisible roads.

There was nothing in my way and no one to bother me.

There was only the lake, open and empty — the swimming area somewhere on the far opposite shore, the NO SWIMMING sign stuck out there somewhere in the middle, obscured by the sunlight that dappled the water's flat surface. And in the distance on the right, the dam wall curved high above the lake. There was a viewing platform up there that we had visited on a school field trip. You could push a button and listen to Finkle's voice explaining about hydro-electricity and irrigation and the future of the region. About the catchment up in the mountains that fed the water through giant pipes all the way down to the power station up the river, where the engineers and the computers decided how much water had to go where, and when it had to go there. You could *ooh* and *aah* about the grandeur of his vision and the invisible weight of history.

Or you could turn around, toward the lake, and think about the weight of water on top of your town.

Part of me wanted to swim out toward it, out into the center, to put my head down and just keep going and going, and see where I ended up.

Instead, I hugged the shoreline, swimming parallel with the bank.

I did my six and probably another six as well.

Maybe more. It was hard to tell.

There were no ladders or flags up here, no big black numbers reminding me how far I'd come, how far I still had to go. There was no wall to slap and turn around and rinse-repeat, again and again. There were no cannonballs or tennis balls or sudden waves of water slapping me in the face.

It made me want to go farther. It made me feel like I could.

I swam until my arms hummed, until my legs began to ache and drag through the water behind me, until I could no longer ignore the ragged rise and fall of my chest in its rattling cage.

Then I sat in the shallows, willing my breathing to slow, to smooth itself out. I let my legs sink heavily into the warm mud and looked out across the lake.

You couldn't see the other side, not really. You could pretend you did — tell yourself that a quick flash over there in the distance was a Jet Ski or a speedboat. But the truth was it might just as easily have been a bird swooping low along the water or a speck swimming haphazardly across the surface of your eyeball.

All you could see for certain were the tops of trees, the very tips of things. It was weird, but the water was in the way somehow, stopping me from seeing what I knew was there.

It's funny how water curves. How when you have a still surface and the right kind of angle, it becomes a kind of skin over itself, a bubble reaching and reaching but never quite bursting.

Surface tension our teacher Mr. Chadwick called it last year. He showed us how we could pile coin after coin into an already-full glass without it overflowing. How we could thread a needle into the surface so it would float rather than sink.

There were other things as well. The way water makes light bend, the way it can make something as straight as a rod look twisted and broken. I had stared at my two-step arm, half in and half out of the fish tank.

I hadn't known this about water, that it had all these tricks. When I said that, Mr. Chadwick laughed. He said they weren't exactly tricks. They were experiments. Science.

It seemed tricky to me, though. And it made me feel strange about water, wary. As if your uncle had suddenly pulled a rabbit out of a hat at a party one day, and now you couldn't help watching him out of the corner of your eye, wondering what else he might have lurking up his sleeve.

I blinked in the sunlight and turned my head to make the surface flat again. It was as simple as that.

Then I dragged myself from the mud and headed up the bank toward my towel.

Six

On the way back into town, I rode past the pool, past the yelling and the squealing and the loudspeaker blaring: "No running! No diving! Watch your children at all times! Hot French fries now available at the canteen!"

The chlorine hit my nostrils like a slap. I put my head down and pumped the pedals furiously.

When I came to Country Crafts, halfway up Main Street, I slowed down. What day was it? No, Dad wouldn't be there today. His slots were Monday and Saturday, sometimes Thursday during peak season, when the town's population doubled for a month over summer and the streets filled with people you'd never seen before and would never see again.

Those were the days he came in and worked on the wheel, demonstrating and chatting to customers, quietly selling them things without them even realizing it.

The people who ran the shop liked to keep things organized. It wasn't like the old days. I'd seen photos of Dad back then — straggly beard, rolled-up sleeves, hands plunged deep into the clay, part of the messy gaggle of artists who came and went as they pleased in the sprawling wooden building.

I wheeled my bike across the street. Some of Dad's work was featured in the window, and there were a couple of small pots sitting just outside on a display shelf. I picked one up. It might be a vase or a potpourri holder. Or maybe just something that would sit on a shelf somewhere and look arty. Dad said sometimes he just let the clay do what it wanted, let it run through his fingers and find its own shape. Then he let the tourists decide, smiling as they turned his work over in their hands and said, *What an interesting cup* or *I love the design of this paperweight.*

I remembered this piece. I remembered the glaze Dad had used. I had been on my way down the hall to hang my towel when he called out to me. The afternoon sun was streaming through the window behind him, making him look like a man on fire.

"What do you think, Cass?" he said. "Blue? Or maybe green?"

I shook my head. "Red."

"Hmm, okay." He smiled, nodded. As if I knew what I was talking about. As if I had a good reason for choosing it, rather than just liking the warm glow the day had set around him.

And now here it was. A red something — on a shelf outside the shop. Waiting for someone to come along and tell it what to be.

I leaned my bike against the wall and stared at the piece. I had never quite gotten used to this. It was weird seeing something that had started out as a lump of shapeless clay turn bit by bit — under his hands and on the wheel and in the kiln — into something else completely, something that would make people stop in their tracks on Main Street. It made me look differently at everything around me. It made me wonder about the invisible hands that were behind it all, out of sight.

Footsteps slowed behind me, and I half turned toward the street. It was probably someone wanting to check out the display. I should put this back, get out of the way.

But as I leaned toward the shelf, an arm came around from behind me. A hand gripped my wrist. Firmly.

I looked up. It was a man, shaking his head. A man I knew. A man everyone knew — in the way everyone knows everyone in this kind of town, but in another way as well. From photos and headlines and whispers behind hands.

That poor man. What a terrible thing. And that boy . . . oh.

That poor man? It was his fault! He was lucky they didn't lock him up.

Surely he's suffered enough? A terrible mistake. He'll regret it for the rest of his life.

Well, he should! That poor woman. Those poor boys.

What a thing. What a terrible thing.

"It's okay," I began. "I was just —"

He shook his head again. Or rather, kept shaking it.

He had been bobbing it back and forth the whole time, almost rhythmically, as if he'd gotten caught in a loop and had forgotten how to stop.

And all the while his eyes were locked on Dad's pot, and his fingers clenched tighter around my wrist. Something in it was beginning to throb, like a bruise, and I felt my grip slipping.

If anyone else had grabbed me like that, I would have yelled or pushed back. Maybe taken their hand and peeled the fingers off me one by one.

But it wasn't just anyone. It was *this* man, and his head was shaking and his face was flushed, and I didn't know how to make it better without making it worse, so I did nothing. I stood there out in front of Country Crafts and watched Dad's pottery slip from my fingers and shatter on the sidewalk.

"Dad!" There were more footsteps, running this time. "It's all right. Let go!"

I turned toward the sound of the voice. Wet hair, long shorts, one hand holding them up, the other reaching toward us.

Liam.

"It's all right," he repeated. But he wasn't talking to me. His eyes were locked on his father's face.

I felt the fingers loosen their grip, watched the tension drain from his body.

"Sorry," Liam began. "I —"

A bell jangled as the shop door burst open.

"Cassie?" It was Ellen, who worked the cash register. She stared down at the ground, at the pieces.

Liam's face flushed, and he put a steadying hand on his father's arm. "It wasn't . . ." he began. "He —"

"Sorry," I said quickly. "I was just looking. It slipped."

I bent down to pick up the jagged fragments. Some were almost smooth, whole in themselves, as if they were pieces of a puzzle that could be snapped back together at any moment. But others were shattered, crushed.

Ellen frowned. "Is that one of your dad's?"

"Yeah. Sorry."

She gestured to a sign on the door. "Well, you know the rules. You break it, you've bought it."

"Okay."

Ellen looked across at Liam and his dad. "Did you guys want something?"

"I have a package!" Liam's father said suddenly, a smile breaking across his face. He reached into the bag that was slung over his shoulder and pulled out a thick envelope. "Here."

Ellen brightened. "Oh, good. I've been waiting for that." She took the envelope from his hands. On the front it read: *Country Crafts. Centenary Brochures,* in black marker. The handwriting was familiar, and so was the logo in the corner of the envelope: a cluster of tall trees around a lake, ringed by the words *New Lower Grange, Growing the Future.*

It was Hannah's writing, a package from the town council.

Ellen turned to take it inside. "Well, I'd better get on with it." She waved a hand at me, at the broken pieces in my palm. "Don't worry about it this time, Cass. Just be careful, okay?"

I nodded. "Thanks."

She smiled and gestured at my wet hair. "Do your six?"

"Um, yeah." I flushed.

She was only being friendly, but sometimes I got tired of everyone knowing my business. Sometimes I wished the town was bigger. I found myself looking forward to summer, when the tourists arrived and I could slip unnoticed through streets full of strangers.

As the door jangled behind Ellen, Liam exhaled next to me, a long shaft of air that made me realize he must have been holding his breath.

"Thanks," he said. "My dad . . . you know, he —"

"It's okay," I said.

It felt wrong, talking about his dad like that when he was right there. He was a bit slow sometimes. He got confused. But he understood stuff. And he was Liam's dad.

Liam turned to him. "Have you got anything else to deliver?"

His father shook his head. "Weeding the gardens now." His speech was blurry, slow, as if he'd just been woken from a deep sleep.

"You want me to walk you back?" Liam pointed up the street to where the town hall sat at the top of the hill, overlooking the town. His father didn't exactly work there. They just gave him odd jobs, the kind of things he could do when he was having a good day. The kind of jobs where it wouldn't matter if he got distracted along the way and sat in the town square for half an hour watching the hands on the clock tower turn.

"Yes. Good." His father nodded.

Liam turned to me. "Thanks for not telling. He needs the job."

"That's okay." I tipped the broken pieces into the front pocket of my bag, listening to them clatter dully down on top of one another. "He really didn't like that pot."

"It's not that," Liam began. "It's just —"

"I was kidding," I said quickly. I pulled one pigtail around to the front and squeezed droplets of water out onto the sidewalk.

Liam stared down at the dark patches on the sidewalk, then up at me. "You told Ellen you did your six."

I shrugged. "Yeah."

"I just came from the pool. I didn't see you."

"Oh?" I fiddled absently with the zipper on my backpack. "You must have missed me. I'm always there."

"I know. That's why . . ." He trailed off. "Never mind."

He nodded toward his father, who had begun shuffling slowly up the street. "I'd better get going."

"Yeah, me too. Hang my towel and stuff."

"Okay, so . . . see you at school, then." He paused. "Maybe I'll catch you at the pool after?"

"Yeah, maybe."

As Liam hurried to catch up with his father, I went over and retrieved my bike. Then I jumped on the pedals and headed away down the hill, glad to be going in the opposite direction so he couldn't see my face.

Seven

"Hang your towel?"

"Yep."

Mom and Hannah were at the kitchen table, staring at the screen of Hannah's laptop.

Dad was in the studio with the door closed, which meant one of two things — either he was doing detail work on his plates and didn't want to be interrupted or he was working on one of his wacky heads and didn't want Mom to see.

"It's coming together," Hannah said. "See?"

I leaned between them and watched as she scrolled slowly through the pages she had laid out on the screen.

On the Move

A Town Reborn

New Beginnings

Out with the Old, In with the New

Lower Grange Says Yes! to Progress

"It looks good," I said. And it did. It was slick and professional. There were clean, crisp borders around the scanned photos and newspaper clippings. The text Hannah had added wrapped over and between them in a way that looked right, as if the pages hadn't been put together by someone but had always been there. There was something strange, though. I couldn't put my finger on it at first, but as Hannah scrolled further and further, past smiling faces and tall, leafy trees, I realized.

All the headlines were happy and shiny, all about progress and improvement and sparkling new swimming pools.

"Where's the rest?" I asked.

Hannah frowned. "What do you mean?"

"You know," I said. "About the protests and everything."

I had read about it, back when I was *Mom's little historian*. About the arguments and the angry town meetings.

It hadn't all been happy and shiny, the way it was on the screen.

Some people had been furious about it. They had fought to keep the town, at least at first.

There were groups formed to protect historical buildings and the old trees in the surrounding forest and the anteater and the not-very-common orchid that someone might possibly have seen once in the bush just west, or maybe east, of town.

Protesters parked themselves on the platform at the top of the old fire lookout tree. For a few weeks, Elijah made extra pocket money climbing up and down the spiral peg ladder, carrying food and water on the way up and foul-smelling buckets on the way down.

It didn't last. Because in the end, the engineers and the politicians all agreed. Lower Grange had to go.

The settlers hadn't thought it through, you see. Eighty-eight years earlier, they had thought it was the perfect spot for a town. They hadn't realized it was actually the perfect spot for a dam that would irrigate the whole region, the whole bustling network of towns and farms that would come along years later and grow bigger and busier and more water-hungry than Lower Grange itself would ever be. It was progress, and you couldn't stand in the way of it. If you did, you'd get swallowed by a giant wall of water.

Hannah shot me a look. "I know about all that stuff, Cass. I was *there*, remember? It's a matter of choosing what's most important." She scrolled idly back and forth with the mouse. "I think we're pretty much set now. We've narrowed it down to what we need."

I nodded. Not because I agreed but because I knew what she was talking about. Someone getting to choose. Somebody narrowing things down. It was like Mom was always telling her classes. I had seen her scrawling it across their essays in her wild, looping handwriting: *Dig deeper. Remember — history is written by the winners!*

Or maybe it was like me telling Ellen that I was sorry. That I was just looking, that Dad's pottery had slipped.

Each of those things was true. But put together, they

didn't tell the real story. There were cracks in between where important stuff leaked out. It's a funny thing, an unsettling thing—how you can tell the truth and have it still be a lie.

"Yeah," I began, "but what about . . . ?" I stopped. There was a crunch of gravel as a car came around the bend into our driveway much too fast.

Tourists! I thought. It was hard to see through the shower of dirt and tiny stones thrown up as the car braked outside, but I knew that's who it would be. They come out here accidentally sometimes, taking a wrong turn on their way to the tearoom. They flatten the tiny wildflowers on the side of the road, spray dust all over Mom's hanging laundry, then get cranky with us because we're not a genuine copy of a rustic historical cottage serving Devonshire tea.

There was a loud banging on the front door. I leaned back on my chair and looked down the hall. That way, I wouldn't even have to get up. I could just yell directions to Ye Olde Tearoom and tell them no, we absolutely definitely could not just whip them up a batch of country-style scones.

Instead, the door to the studio swung open, and

Dad elbowed his way into the hall like a surgeon going into an operation, his hands slick with clay.

"Howard!" he said. "Come in, come in."

I stared down the hall. Finkle? What was he doing here?

That man really was everywhere.

There was a photo of him right there on the screen, one that looked like it had been taken about twenty years ago, when he still had hair. He was resting his chin on one balled-up fist, evidently trying to appear thoughtful. There was a caption underneath: "Howard Finkle, Centenary Mayor."

"Hello, girls!" he called down the hall. Then he clapped Dad on the back and followed him into the studio, the door slamming shut behind them.

That was when I realized.

Finkle's oddly crooked nose — not unlike a random blob of mashed clay that could possibly be something someone had left there by accident.

I turned to Hannah. She was grinning.

"Commemorative sculpture," she said. "Also my idea. Howard loves it. Dad loves it. Everybody wins."

Mom sighed. "Not if Dad doesn't get all his pots

finished in time for the tourist season. I can't believe you've got him making a free head right before the busy season, Hannah."

Hannah clicked the mouse impatiently, making the screen blur. "I told you, Mom — it's not really free. It'll be great publicity. We've got big plans for the centenary. There'll be people coming down from the city — newspapers, TV, the whole thing. And Elijah will be back soon. He can help with the pots."

As she stopped talking, Hannah stopped clicking. The screen snapped back into focus, and I leaned down toward it. The book was in thumbnail view now, showing everything at once. My page was in the middle somewhere, surrounded by pictures of the pool and Country Crafts and the newly sealed Main Street. Somewhere near the top of the screen was a photo of Finkle with a lever in his hand.

And off to one side, something else.

I drew in a quick breath.

It was another newspaper clipping, dated a few months earlier than mine. There was another grainy photo — another tired couple, two more small bundles. Underneath were paragraphs of closely typed text.

I leaned across Hannah and clicked on the magnifying-glass icon to blow them up: "newborn tragedy," "local man in hospital," "possible brain damage," "cause unclear," "fatigue may be a factor," "driver error likely, say police." Above them, the headline read: "Miracle Baby Survives Crash."

Hannah followed my gaze. "He's in your class, isn't he?"

I nodded, peering forward. "Is this going in, too?"

Hannah shook her head. "No, that's just something I found when I was going through some other stuff." She tapped a finger repeatedly on the keyboard, enlarging Liam's miracle-baby face until it filled the screen, huge and pixelated. "No point dredging all that up again. Not now that everyone's moved on."

I glared at her. Moved on? I couldn't help but picture Liam's curious gait, his too-long shorts; could almost feel, suddenly, the tightening grip of his father's hand on my wrist.

I reached for the mouse. "It's time for dinner."

"Wait!" Panic flashed across Hannah's face. "I haven't saved it!"

"It's okay," I said. "I'm only putting it on sleep."

She nodded. "What a surprise."

Elijah always used to tell me off for never shutting down the computer completely. He said it wasn't good for it, that things need the chance to switch right off and then start again clean. But I couldn't help myself. There was something about sleep mode that I found irresistible. I loved the way it suspended everything just the way it was. How everything went dark and quiet and still, but when you opened it up, it snapped back into life, all of it right there, just waiting for the light.

I stared down at the computer. Then I clicked the button once, twice, and watched Liam's face disappear as the screen faded to black.

Eight

Thunkity-thunk. Thunkity-thunk.

I didn't look up from the mosaic. This was a tricky bit, snipping the blue tiles just right so they would fit into the outline I'd traced for Tucker's Supermarket. We each had a section to work on, and when they were done, we were going to piece them all together like a giant floor puzzle. It was important to get the edges right, to follow the template so it all worked, so everything would fit the way it was supposed to.

But even without looking, I knew what the familiar *thunkity-thunk* was. For me, this was the sound track to every school day — Liam's feet kicking rhythmically at my chair from the desk behind.

It had annoyed me at first. I used to turn around and tell him to stop. He would for a while, but then it would start up once more, and when I turned around again, he would look surprised, like he hadn't realized, like his legs had simply taken on a life of their own.

After a while, I stopped saying anything. A while later, I stopped minding.

After a longer while, I kind of started liking it.

It got so that if he was away, I missed it. It was like a background hum you don't even realize is there until it's gone and the air around you feels empty all of a sudden.

In some ways, that was true about Liam, too.

It wasn't that we were friends or anything — at least not particularly. It was just that he had always been around. We used to run into him at the hospital when I was little and still going in for my checkups. I remember sitting with him in the corner of the waiting room, building unsteady worlds out of blocks while our mothers sat straight-backed along the wall, leafing through old magazines to pass the time. Later, at school, we sat out of PE together, shredding leaf after leaf in the shade of the spreading eucalyptus while other kids ran and jumped and hurled themselves at things.

Every now and then, a ball would come our way, or a bored boundary fielder would take a few extra steps backward to strike up a conversation.

Liam would always look up. He'd grab the ball and throw it back in a long, swooping arc. He'd say, *How's it going?* and *What's the score?* and *Heads up! Here comes a long one.*

But I would keep my head down, the way I always did, keep my eyes on my leaf, concentrating on shearing a clean, smooth line right down the center of the spine.

Now, though, I looked up. I stopped my pliers midsnip and stared over at the door to the classroom. Because someone was coming in. Someone familiar. Someone with an oddly crooked nose.

"Good morning, children!" Finkle was holding a wooden box. A display case with something inside it, nestled snugly between velvet pillows.

He smiled, a broad, Cheshire cat grin as if all our wildest dreams had suddenly come true and he was the dazzling messenger of them. "Yes, that's right," he said. "It is what you think it is. Can you believe it?"

I couldn't.

It was the lever. The actual lever.

From her desk, Mrs. Barber nodded. "From the *archives*." She said the last word in a whisper, as if it was a secret.

Finkle nodded solemnly. Then he passed the lever around the room so we could take turns holding it, so we could *feel the solid weight of history in the very palms of our hands*.

As we did, he told us all about his artistic vision, which involved our mosaic, his lever, and a whole lot of weirdness.

The lever wasn't only here for inspiration. It was also so we could make sure it fit. So we could mold our hundreds of tiles around it.

It was coming out of the archives and going into our mosaic. Mosaics plural, in fact. There were two of them.

One for Old Lower Grange. One for New.

They were going to lie side by side in the city

square, with the lever in between, surrounded by a decorative border.

"A sundial!" Finkle boomed, as if he was announcing the most important announcement in the entire history of announcements. Then he picked up a marker and drew a sketch on the board.

New Lower Grange was going to be a sundial, with compass points directing tourists to places of vibrant and/or laid-back interest.

Old Lower Grange was going to be a water feature, with a drinking fountain on one end.

The town would sit underwater, and when the level dropped too low, you could flip the lever, releasing more water into the well, drowning the old town over and over again.

I told myself not to think about whether it was morbid or festive.

After Finkle left, I studied my growing pile of blue. That should be enough for now. It was only the new Tucker's that was blue. For the old one, I needed some orange and yellow from the pile up front.

I pushed my chair back and stood up.

"Ow!"

Behind me, Liam had one foot tangled in my chair leg.

"Sorry." I looked down at his desk. He was snipping tiles for the fire tree — green and brown, green and brown. The fire tree was an enormous, ancient eucalyptus tree that used to act as a fire lookout for the area. It had metal spikes running all the way up it like a kind of spiral ladder, and a platform at the top where someone would sit, looking out over the bush for telltale curls of smoke. It was one of the easiest sections of the mosaic — first, because it was pretty much just a tall, straight stick, and second, because there was no "after." They couldn't exactly rebuild a tree, and it would take hundreds of years to grow one even close to tall enough.

Liam hardly had anything to do, really, but Mrs. Barber said it didn't matter. She said he should just take his time and do a really good job of the fire tree.

She said that because she had accidentally almost given him the clock tower. It was the only other section left by the time she got to Liam, and I saw panic flood her face when she realized.

Mrs. Barber shoved the photograph onto her

clipboard and took it back to her desk, where I saw her studying it later.

She was working on it herself. It was easier that way.

That way she didn't have to look Liam in the eye and say the words "clock tower," and we could all get on with piecing New Lower Grange together and pretending none of it had ever happened.

All of us except me.

Maybe it was seeing his dad the other day. Maybe it was passing the pool every day on my way back from the lake and seeing those familiar shorts flapping on the other side of the fence. Maybe it was going back through my box and finding all those old clippings — "Tragic Accident" and "Local Man in Coma" and "Crash Case Continues" — all those articles that couldn't possibly be used because the centenary was a time for celebration and moving forward, and no one wanted to think about that.

I couldn't stop thinking about it.

I couldn't stop seeing the clear night, the clock tower, the car crashing and rolling and burning.

It was probably all wrong, what I was imagining. No one could say for sure what happened. There hadn't exactly been anyone there who was able to describe it later.

Only Liam's dad in a coma.

Liam, two doors down the hall from him, mending his bones and his burns.

And his brother, farther down again, under a thin white sheet, a wall of expensive machines fallen quiet by his side.

Liam untangled his leg. "What?"

I realized I was staring. "Nothing."

I began to turn back around, but then he spoke softly. "Hey, where've you been, anyway?"

"What do you mean? Here." I pointed at my chair. "There."

I knew that wasn't what he meant. He had seen me a couple of times. He might have called out to me once as I was passing the pool, but it was hard to be sure with all the yelling and squealing and announcements about hot fries.

He peered up at me through his bangs, with a little smile that said, *You know and I know that's not what I'm talking about.*

"The pool," he said. "You haven't been going."

"Yes, I have," I began. "I —"

"No, you haven't. I looked."

It was so unexpected that at first I didn't know what to say. My mind raced, hunting for ways to explain. "Oh, you mean the laps," I said finally, as lightly as I could manage. "I don't have to do them anymore. I'm . . . I'm better now."

Liam stared at me. "Really?" he said. "That's great."

I nodded. "Yeah. So . . ." I began to turn back around, then stopped.

Because this was a small town and there was a good chance Liam's mother had a friend whose cousin's sister worked with Mom. All it would take was for Liam to casually say something like "Cassie Romano's finally stopped doing those laps," and within twenty-four hours the hairline cracks in my story would have spread and spread until they split everything wide open.

I glanced back over my shoulder and kept my voice light, as if it was an afterthought. "Could you . . . could you not tell anyone? About the laps."

"About you being better?" Liam raised his eyebrows. "Yeah."

He hesitated a second, then nodded.

"Thanks," I said quietly, but his head was already bent over the desk. I headed for the front, picking my way in between the tile fragments scattered here and there so as not to grind them into the carpet.

I gathered orange and yellow tiles from the box, looking across all the while toward my desk, toward Liam, his head bent low over his pieces.

As I watched, he brought his hammer down hard into the center of a light-brown tile, shattering it into a pile of uneven pieces.

Beneath my hands, I felt the cool, slick surface of the tiles. It was a strange idea when you thought about it — smashing something so you could piece it back together.

Nine

I didn't miss an afternoon at the lake.

When the bell rang at the end of the school day, the town kids veered left toward Main Street and the farm kids went right toward the bus stop. And I doubled back along the fence, heading for the break in the trees. From there I could cut across the hills, zigging and zagging until I met up with the path I'd begun to etch back into the hillside, with the warning signs I barely saw anymore, with the hole in the fence I'd learned to knit back up so it couldn't be found by anyone who didn't already know it was there.

I never thought about skipping my swim, the way I used to with the pool. Not even when the temperature soared and the hill seemed steeper than ever and the bush around me felt so dry it might ignite at any moment out of sheer desperation.

It wasn't just the absence of Band-Aids. It wasn't just the quiet. It was the way swimming up there made me want to go farther and faster and harder, the way it didn't feel like doing my six or digging in, but just like cruising across the surface.

And maybe it was also something else, something I wasn't quite letting myself think about, something I had shoved years ago into a box under my bed.

Something that lay far below, something I didn't realize was about to come rising up to meet me.

On the last day of school, we finished our essays. I crumpled up the one that began "My Lower Grange is two hundred feet underwater" and tossed it in the trash.

We finished our handprints. I chipped jagged bits of clay from the edges of my fingers, then smoothed over the rough bits with a slick layer of spit.

And we finished our mosaics. I closed the doors on Tucker's. Liam pegged all the way to the top of the fire tree. Amber added the last square of blue to the lake.

It looked nothing like the lake, that color. As I stood

in the shallows that afternoon, it wasn't blue I saw. It was a hundred mixed-up shades of brown and blue and green, all of them blending into something you could never reproduce with a bunch of smashed-up tiles. And none of what was visible on the surface told you anything about what was underneath, about the bands of warm and cool, light and dark, that led you down to where the chill lay at the bottom, settled over the mud and the silt like a heavy blanket.

I pushed off across the water and began my swim. I was trying to practice breathing on the left as well as the right. Mr. Henshall always said we should, but I always got muddled on the left and ended up with a mouthful of water.

Breathe right, stroke-stroke, breathe left, stroke-stroke, breathe right, stroke-stroke. Slowly, I settled into an awkward rhythm, following the line of the shore as it curved away to the east.

Breathe right, stroke-stroke, breathe left, stro . . . what?

As I turned, there was a flash of something, something cutting through the glare of light slicing off the water.

It was nothing, probably. A spot on my goggles.

Breathe right, stroke-stroke . . .

Funny, though. The spot wasn't there when I breathed right.

Which made it not a spot.

I breathed left slowly this time. Just to be sure that there was nothing. That it had been, if not a randomly appearing goggle-spot, then some kind of trick of the light, a reflection off the surface of the water.

But there it was again, that flash.

I gulped a mouthful of lake water, brackish and dark, and stopped, treading water. Leaned forward and squinted.

There was definitely something.

Something that hadn't been there yesterday.

Not a fish. Or a bird. It wasn't moving.

It was long and kind of straight. It looked . . . sticky.

I snickered to myself. It was my favorite joke when I was little. *What's brown and sticky? A stick!* Ha.

It did look like a stick. But it was deep out there. Too deep for it to be a stick all on its own. There would have to be something holding it up.

A hand! I couldn't help imagining it — a long arm

beneath the surface, a pale white hand rising up to offer me this stick.

That would be just my luck, to land in the middle of a mythical adventure, and instead of a magic unbreakable sword that will give me dominion over many lands and make me a figure of legend for generations to come, I get a stick.

Was it really a stick?

I leaned farther forward.

It wasn't that far away. It wasn't in the middle of the lake or anything. Maybe three hundred feet?

Three hundred feet there, check out the whatever-it-was, three hundred feet back.

Not even six laps.

Easy.

It was deep out there, of course. Deeper than here. And here was deeper than where I normally swam. When I stretched a leg down, a foot, then a toe, as far as it could go, I still couldn't touch the bottom.

But that didn't matter.

I'd never understood the big deal about deep water. If you can swim, you can swim. It doesn't matter what's underneath as long as you can get to the other side.

I put my head down and set off, breathing and stroking, breathing and stroking.

After a couple of minutes, I looked up. I figured I must be just about on top of the thing, and I didn't want to crash into it, especially if it was a sword that was going to give me dominion over many lands.

Except . . . where was it?

I swiveled my head. Had I swum off course? I should have thought of that. It was easy to do in open water. Mr. Henshall had warned us about it, said we should always line ourselves up with something and keep checking our direction.

That's what the stick thing was for, if only I could find it.

There was something over there, but that couldn't be it. It didn't seem any bigger, any closer at all.

But it must be that. What else could it be, this far out? It just didn't seem to be getting any closer, even though I'd swum all this way.

How far had I come, actually?

That was something else that was hard to measure without flags and black marks and people whacking you randomly with tennis balls.

I looked back toward the shore, then out at the stick thing.

Okay, so it was more than three hundred feet. It would still be all right. I had probably been doing way more than that the last few weeks. I felt good. I felt strong.

I kept going, lifting my head every few strokes to stay in line with the stick.

It was getting bigger now, definitely.

Slowly, though. More slowly than I'd expected.

Too slowly.

When I started thinking about it — how far I'd come, how far I might have to go — I felt a familiar tightening in my chest. My breath started coming in short, ragged bites.

With every stroke, Mr. Henshall was in my head. Don't try to judge distances in open water. Line yourself up with something. Don't overestimate your ability. *Stroke-stroke-breathe, stroke-stroke-breathe.*

I swam the last few feet, which was probably more like sixty, in a grandma breaststroke.

Partly it was so I could keep my eyes locked onto the stick thing, so it wouldn't disappear.

Mostly it was because I was exhausted.

I was past the point of digging in.

And I was remembering, all of a sudden, the crucial thing about deep water. That it doesn't matter as long as you can get to the other side. But there was no other side here, not that I could reach, and depth was, in fact, quite important when you've grossly underestimated distance and need somewhere to reach down to with a leg, a foot, a toe.

Because there's nothing to hang on to. Nothing but water and sky and something you haven't quite managed to identify yet.

There it was, right in front of me.

It was indeed sticky. It was indeed a stick thing.

For a second I stopped, imagining the hand holding it up, the arm reaching all the way from the bottom of the lake.

Then I shook my head.

Because I was an idiot.

It was a stick thing in its natural habitat. In the middle of a lake, yes. But also at the top of a tree.

And a tree was something to hold on to for a little while. A tree might have a branch where you could perch and wait for a bit, gathering yourself for the much-longer-than-expected swim back.

My toe brushed something, and I jumped. Then I sent my toe back down again for another feel, because this was what I was after, wasn't it — a branch, something I could stand on?

A wide, flat branch, even. A branch wider and flatter, in fact, than any branch ever before found in nature.

Which was weird until I realized:

Not a branch, but a platform.

A platform at the top of the tallest tree in Old Lower Grange, in the whole county. A platform with a peg ladder spiraling below it all the way down to the silty mud.

The fire tree!

I felt around with my toes. It was definitely a platform, going right around the trunk. The wood was rotting and falling away, but the metal frame was still there, and it was enough for me to rest my feet on so I could lean back against the tree and close my eyes, just for a second, and rest and breathe.

I was here. I was somewhere.

Ten

When my breathing had slowed, I took a long look around me. I inched around the metal frame with my toes, felt the slippery bark around the trunk with my fingers.

The fire tree! How did it get here? I mean, not how did it *get* here. That was quite possibly the world's dumbest question. Obviously, it had been here all along, for hundreds of years, in fact, growing and growing and slowly leaving behind everything around it while it reached for the sky.

But still, how did it get *here*?

Up into the actual sky above the water? And how had I never noticed it before?

I looked back the way I had come, across to the shoreline, where my orange towel sat flapping on a low-hanging tree branch.

And I saw something. A dark stain around the lake, a line along the water's edge like you see at the ocean when the tide has gone out.

Except that there were no tides at the lake.

My eyes flicked from the water to my towel and back again, from the water to the tree line and back again.

And then I realized.

Something that should have been obvious days ago, maybe even weeks ago.

The water level was going down. It had been a dry winter, a dry few years, and now summer was sinking its teeth in, and the lake was, well, sinking.

It was lower than I'd ever seen it.

That meant water restrictions over the summer. It meant watering one day a week and Mom sticking an egg timer in the shower.

But it meant something else, too.

It meant this tree, the old fire tree — the stuff of

photos and stories and a hundred crayon drawings —
was suddenly reaching up from the deep with its
spindly fingers.

I stared down through the water at my feet, at the
platform, at the pegs that spiraled down and down into
the dark.

Old Lower Grange was down there. It had always
been there, but now it was right below me. Now I was
standing on something that was actually connected to
it, something I had seen in photos and heard about in
stories, and there was a road, right here, leading down,
saying, *Come on.*

How deep could it be?

How far could it be?

How far?

A thought lodged in my throat like a stone.

I looked out across the water, all the way to the
shoreline, and my heart sank.

It was so far. It seemed obvious now. Maybe it was
because I'd already swum it once. Maybe it was because
the shore was bigger and wider and made it easier to
get a sense of things.

It didn't matter why. It was a long way. Just getting here I'd probably swum farther than I ever had before.

But I didn't feel like patting myself on the back for that.

I was bigger now and stronger, but I was still an idiot.

I was in Old Lower Grange, where the water was dropping to meet the town. I was on top of the fire tree. From here, I could dive down into my own secret Atlantis.

But right now, all I could think about was how I was going to make it back to shore.

It was getting late. I needed to be over there. I needed to be on the shore, pulling on my socks and my shoes, bumping my way back down the hill.

It would be easier this time, I told myself. It was always easier on the way back, when you knew you didn't have to turn around and do the whole thing again.

I would breaststroke it. Maybe some sidestroke. Survival strokes, Mr. Henshall called them.

That seemed like a goal worth aiming for — survival.

I would keep my head up and my stroke *long and slow and relaxed.* I would have Mr. Henshall in my head and my eyes fixed on my bright-orange towel, all the way over there in the distance, and I would swim absolutely straight, adding not one extra foot to the left or right.

I pushed off from the tree.

The tiredness returned almost immediately — not the welcome buzzing in my limbs I felt after a good, hard swim, but a deadening heaviness.

I put it out of my mind.

I would think about something else. My arms and legs knew what to do all on their own. So I would take my mind somewhere else, and before I knew it, I'd be all the way over there.

Old Lower Grange. That was it. I would swim it as if I were walking the streets of the old town, and they would carry me out.

I called up the mosaic, the maps piled in layers in the box under my bed.

The fire tree behind me, the shore ahead. And the sun — which way was the sun? That put the dam wall to the east, the bike path to the south.

In my head, the map spun and turned, roads and buildings bumping from slot to slot. It was a puzzle — that was it — one of those frames with the little plastic tiles you move around piece by piece until the picture snaps into focus.

New Lower Grange southeast, to the right of the hill. The fire tree kind of north.

And me, swimming south. South-ish.

So that would put me somewhere near the bakery, Il Panino. If I turned right, I'd be heading toward school. Left, and I'd hit the old sawmill.

Straight ahead, and I'd pass through the playground and the second bakery whose name I always forgot and the barber's.

I floated over the top of them all, heading for the town square, seeing it laid out below me in a thousand colorful pieces.

Long and slow and relaxed.

Just head for the orange.

Past the town square now, over the clock tower, where I would not think about fiery crashes and tiny Liam in the backseat, all curled-up fingers and toes, not knowing that everything in his brand-new world was already about to change. On up to the rambling old house that would become Country Crafts, where his father would one day grip my wrist so tightly it hurt. Then down Main Street to where bakery number three would soon make way for our sparkling, safe, and Band-Aid-filled pool.

How far was that now? Half the town? I looked out to the shore and then back at the tree. My heart lifted. More than halfway. Maybe three-quarters.

But it was so slow, this grandma breaststroke. I was getting cold and tired.

I had to get there.

I nodded to myself. I would swim the rest. I would keep my head down and get it over and done with quickly. A few more minutes and I'd be there.

I kicked off and reached back for the first stroke. *Long and easy,* I began. *Long and —*

Suddenly, my breath caught in my throat. There was a sharp pain in my thigh, as if something had grabbed it. It stopped kicking, wouldn't do what I told it. It hung there flapping, wooden and sluggish and throbbing with pain.

I was so heavy all of a sudden, so useless. I couldn't

breathe, couldn't get a breath. Which side was I turning? Which way?

I turned my head, flailing, and sucked in a deep gulp, but it was water I got instead of sky, instead of air.

I was going under, felt myself start to go, my leg dragging me down, and I waited, reaching for something, anything, with my good leg and my foot and the ends of my toes.

But there was nothing. It was too deep, and my head was going under, the water closing, knitting itself back together above me. And I was an idiot, because for a second I thought I saw someone running, waving, coming across the water, mouth open, shouting.

But there was no one, and I knew that. People don't run, don't wave, don't make their way to you across the water.

I was under, and my mouth was open, taking in great gulps of lake like it was oxygen, and I thought, *Oh, a pool is good; it's safe and convenient; it has lifeguards.* And then, *Work, leg, work,* but it wouldn't, and if Mr. Henshall had been there, it would have listened, because everyone listens to him, even when he doesn't make any kind of sense.

And it's crazy the things you see, you think, when you're going under, because there was someone and Mr. Henshall and *Work, leg, work,* but it wouldn't. And as the water folded me down into itself, there were flashes of color, *of blue or maybe green or maybe a kind of greeny-blue, and what do you call that in-between color, anyway? And a mosaic with jagged edges — should have trimmed them, careless.* And I wondered if this is what you see, if this is what you think when you're sinking, when you're going under all the way down into the silty dark, and how I wish, I wish I had a sword that gave me dominion over the lands.

Or even just a stick.

A stick.

Oh, a stick, up there in the light.

The good light.

Following me down.

My fingers, finding it.

That voice yelling, that mouth open, rushing toward me.

A platform up above me, something to grab on to, something to clamber onto, something to be safe.

So I tried, dragging my traitor leg behind me like a broken wing, and he leaned out toward me, held the stick, said, *holdonjustholdonthat'sall;* said, *Stay back, Cassie. I'm serious. Don't make me break your nose.*

Eleven

That was from Mr. Henshall as well.

Don't get too close, he always said. *Don't let a drowning person drag you down with them.*

It was most important *to secure your own safety at all times.* It was *reach to rescue* and *defensive posture* and *break their nose if you have to (don't quote me on this).*

I held on to the stick, on to the branch, and I didn't grab on to the platform, which was a raft, of sorts. I let myself be dragged through the water, and then we were in the shallows, and he was hauling me in, all the way to the good solid ground — the voice, the mouth, the someone.

Liam.

I sat in the mud while he pulled the raft up onto the bank.

What are you doing here? I wanted to ask, and *How did you get here?* and *Where did you get that raft thing?* But I couldn't say anything just yet, could only focus on getting air in and out, in and out.

"Are you okay?" Liam sat down near me at the water's edge.

I nodded. I didn't feel okay — not yet — but I knew I would soon. Eventually. Because even though my leg was still wood and there was lake in my throat, I was out now and there wasn't any farther to sink.

"Thanks," I said finally. "My leg — it . . ." I made claws of my hands, gritting my teeth.

"Cramp. I had that in the pool once. The wall was right there, and I thought I wasn't going to make it back. Pretty scary."

"Yeah." I ran one hand cautiously down my leg, probing for the pain.

Cramp? Was that it? Nothing to do with my lungs or digging in, but just a normal cramp, like anyone could get.

Any idiot who tried to swim out into the middle of the lake after a stick, that is.

"You probably just went too far," Liam said. "What were you doing out there?" He peered out across the lake. "What's that thing?"

"The fire tree," I said. "That's where I went."

"The fire tree?" He turned back to me quickly. "Seriously? How far is that?"

"I don't know. A long way."

He gave a low whistle. "You're crazy. I mean, I know you're *better* and everything, but . . ."

I leaned back on my elbows. "I thought it was closer. I thought I could get there. I did get there. Then I had to get back." I shot him a quick look. "How long have you been here, anyway?"

"I only saw you just there." He pointed to a spot about halfway between the shore and the tree. "You were doing the breaststroke. You looked okay. Lucky I had the raft, though."

I stared up the bank. His so-called raft was a row of planks bound together with rotting string and tied to the top of some rusty metal drums.

"Where did you get that thing?" I said. "What are you even doing here?"

Liam pulled at his shorts. From one edge, a thick, raised scar tracked down his leg like a centipede.

"I knew you were swimming somewhere," he said. "That day near the pool . . . your hair was wet." He picked up a stone and skimmed it out across the water. It skipped once, twice, then sank.

"Dad made the raft," he said after a while. "We used to come up here all the time."

"Your dad made that?"

Liam's face clouded. "He's not stupid. He's just —"

"I didn't mean that," I said quickly. "I meant I didn't know you came up here. You and him."

"Oh." Liam picked up a leaf and tore down the center along its knobbly spine. "Well, we don't anymore. Mom said it was better not to remind him. He gets . . . worked up."

I followed his gaze out to the lake, to where the clock tower would be if the map in my head was right.

Liam crushed the leaf in his hand, releasing the sharp smell of eucalyptus, and stood up.

"I'd better go. Mom likes me to stop in, see how he's doing."

"Yeah. I should get back." I rocked forward into a squat, then creaked slowly to my feet.

While I pulled my clothes on, Liam dragged the raft behind a tree a little farther along the shoreline.

"I can't believe this is still in one piece," he said. "Sort of." He grinned as a chunk of rotting wood broke off one side. "I forgot how much I like it here. The pool gets so crowded."

I nodded. "Tell me about it."

He scratched at the ground with the rescue stick, dragging a long wavy line through the dirt. For a moment, I thought he was going to say something, but then he shrugged. He gathered his shorts around him, and I followed him up through the trees toward the fence, where his bike lay, resting against mine.

We rode down the hill in silence, apart from the cicadas and the magpies and the rattle of our bikes over the bumpy path.

As we passed the pool, we slowed, then accelerated.

When we reached the town hall, we pulled up

outside. I straddled my bike while Liam leaned his against the racks out in front.

"Well, I'd better go." He jerked a thumb toward the door.

"Yeah, me too." I scuffed one foot against a pedal. "So . . . thanks."

"It's okay. Um . . . see you tomorrow, maybe?"

"Yeah, maybe."

I kicked the pedals around and pushed down. "Hey, would you really have broken my nose?"

As I began to roll, I heard him laugh quietly. "I don't know," he said. Then more loudly, as I headed off the sidewalk and onto the road: "Probably. Maybe."

When I looked back, he was grinning, watching me go.

Twelve

I was pushing my way up the last big hill when I heard it behind me — the roar of an engine, tires crunching on the dirt road.

Tourists. It had to be. Dad would be in the studio all day, working on Finkle, pretending to work on pots. And Mom and Hannah would be home by now, waiting in the kitchen to ask if I'd hung up my towel.

I moved over, crunching across the sticks and leaves at the side of the road, and waited for the car to pass.

Instead, I heard the engine slow as it pulled up alongside me.

It was a once-green utility vehicle. A now-faded and rusted and falling-apart old truck that none of us could believe kept surviving the trip all the way to the city and back.

"Elijah!"

"Hey, doofus!" He rolled down the window, grinning, then coughed as the dust cloud he'd stirred up hit him in the face.

I scooted my bike over awkwardly. "When did you get back?"

"Just now." He nodded at the backseat, which was full of books and clothes and pillows.

"Haven't you been home yet?"

He shook his head. "I went past the pool—thought I might give you a lift. Didn't see you, though."

"I was probably getting changed."

"Except you're not changed."

I looked down. Stupid. My bathing suit was clearly visible under my shirt.

"I meant . . . I was in the bathroom."

"Oh, okay." He frowned. "Must have just missed you."

"You can give me a lift now."

I climbed off the bike and wheeled it toward the back of the truck.

He raised his eyebrows. "We're basically there, Cass."

He was right. We were. But I suddenly felt like I couldn't go any farther, like all of it had caught up with me at once — the swimming, the sinking, the stick. Not to mention this long, dusty hill.

Elijah opened his door and climbed out. He lifted my bike into the back of the truck, then turned to me. "Are you okay?"

"Yeah. Just tired."

"Do your six?"

"Yep."

"Hang your towel?"

I punched him in the arm. "She still says it, you know."

"Oh, I don't doubt it." He put the car into gear and took off up the hill. "Seriously, Cass. Don't push yourself too hard. You look wrecked."

When we eased into the driveway a minute later, the front door flew open immediately. Mom appeared first, followed by Hannah, then Dad.

"Elijah!" Mom put her hands on her hips. "You should have called ahead!" She was smiling, already moving to the window to drag him out for a hug.

"Does this mean my scones aren't ready yet?" Elijah grinned as he climbed out of the car, unfolding his long frame and stretching his arms above his head while Mom tackled him around the waist.

"I'd make you some," she said. "You know I would."

"Yeah, but then I'd have to eat them."

"True."

"Good thing you teach history, not cooking."

"Cheeky!" Mom ducked her head, then caught sight of me in the passenger seat. "Cass?"

Elijah reached up to haul my bike out of the back. "Yeah, I gave her a lift. From the pool. Right, Cass?"

His lips were curved in the shadow of a smile. I hesitated a second before nodding. "Yeah."

"Do your six?" Mom asked.

Elijah burst out laughing.

Mom stared at him. "What's so funny?"

"Nothing." He grabbed an enormous duffel bag from the back of the truck and hoisted it over one shoulder. "Better hang your towel, mate."

"Yeah." I bit my lip to keep from smiling and headed for the clothesline.

Later, after lasagna and apple pie and nothing at all resembling a Devonshire tea, we sat around the table. Elijah told us about his exams and the house he was living in with six other guys, and how he seriously doubted the truck was going to survive another trip. Hannah told him about the centenary celebrations and showed him the draft of the book she'd printed out to make notes on.

Dad told him about the Finkle head and the pots, and Elijah agreed to help him finish things up and cart them into town. But when he asked Dad to show him Finkle, Dad shook his head.

"Not yet," he said. "It's still . . . developing."

Hannah sighed. "That's one word for it."

Finkle was being difficult, apparently. Or Dad was, depending on how you looked at things.

"He wants me to work from this," Dad said, pulling a folded photograph from his pocket.

Hannah rolled her eyes. "That old thing again?"

Dad nodded. "I know. It hardly even looks like him anymore."

"We keep telling him," Hannah said. "He won't

listen. Says he hasn't changed that much. He's in denial or something."

I peered down at the photo. There were some notes scribbled along the edge in black marker — *Left side best* and *Not really that wrinkly.* The face itself was crisscrossed by a grid of lines that divided it up into tiny squares.

Dad snorted. "He seems to think I can just copy the photo, one square at a time."

He ran a finger across Finkle's crosshatched face. It was like those drawings I used to do when I was little, where you copy a picture square by square onto a new grid. No matter how careful I was, they always came out slightly wonky.

"That's not how it works," Dad said. "You can't just break something down into parts like that. This is art, not construction." He tossed the photo onto the table and leaned back in his chair. "I tried to explain to him — what I like to do is look at the photos, capture the essence of the thing, then put them away and just work from the mind's eye, from the hands."

"That explains a lot, actually," Elijah said. When Dad first started doing heads, he had done one of

Elijah that ended up looking disturbingly like a cross-eyed ferret.

Dad whacked him lightly on the shoulder, then sighed. "I just don't think Finkle really understands the artistic process."

Hannah's jaw clenched a little. "I'm sure he doesn't, Dad. But he means well. Just do your best, would you? We're all working hard on this."

She pointed at the centenary book. Elijah had been working his way through it slowly and had just reached my page.

"Ah," he said. "Welcome to New Lower Grange!"

"Yeah." I flushed.

He flicked back and forth quickly. "Bit surprised I don't get a mention. Defenders of the forest, heroes of the tree — carrier of the poo."

"Elijah!" Mom frowned. "Yuck."

"Yeah, it was." He grinned. "I made sixty bucks, though."

"No one needs to remember that," Hannah said. "They weren't heroes. They were feral weirdos."

"Typical Finkle-spin!" Elijah countered. "They were cool. And they were right. That tree was a landmark."

"Trees grow," Hannah said. "Besides, they have better ways of spotting fires now."

"Yeah, well, I liked the fire tree," Elijah said.

"Me too," I said.

"Come off it, Cassie," Hannah said. "You never even saw it. That tree was dangerous. You could fall right through the pegs if you weren't careful. I can't believe they let anyone climb that thing."

"And I can't believe you were too chicken to climb it." Elijah gave her a scornful look. Then he turned to Mom. "Remember when she got about halfway up and was too scared to move?"

Mom nodded. "Oh, yes. Because I was at the bottom, being told off by a family of Japanese tourists. They asked me if Australian mothers normally let their kids do such risky things." She smiled. "I didn't know what to say."

Elijah went over to the bench and filled the kettle with water. "Yeah, and I couldn't get down because I was already up, and she was so hysterical, she wouldn't let anyone past."

Hannah folded her arms. "I was ten, Elijah."

"Yeah, and I was eight. I couldn't believe it. But that

wasn't the best bit, was it, Mom? Remember how that guy went up to his car . . . ?"

I tuned out the rest of what Elijah was saying. I knew the story. I'd heard it a hundred times. About how an English tourist got a rock-climbing harness from his car and went up after Hannah. He put her into the harness and told her she was safe now, and she climbed all the way down like a monkey, even though he hadn't clipped her to anything at all.

It was supposed to be a lesson on the power of the mind, but when Mom told Hannah later, she just started crying all over again.

"It was so funny." Elijah reached up into the cupboard for the jar of coffee.

"Well," countered Hannah, "what about the time you were coming down the tree and that bucket of . . . stuff . . . tipped all over you?"

Dad laughed. "Yeah, and remember when . . ."

I sighed and leaned back in my chair. That was my cue to switch off—*remember when?* Once they started telling stories, there was no stopping them. They would bounce back and forth across the table for hours. Serve and volley. Volley and return.

And there was never anything for me to do, nothing for me to add, because all of it had happened before I was born, in a place I'd never been.

The only family story about me was from the day I was born, the day I threw the grading and the pottery and everything else you could possibly imagine into disarray by arriving not only accidentally but also way too early.

It was a good story, and Dad told it well.

About how he piled everyone into the Valiant, spinning the tires as they took off and taking a big wounded chunk out of the sod lawn.

How when he saw the fuel light flashing, he pulled into the shiny new gas station. And when he realized it had lots of two-for-the-price-of-one Mars bars, supersize hot-dog deals, and ice-cold slushies, but no actual gas yet, he put his head down on the steering wheel, making the horn blare.

How for a brief, crazy moment, he contemplated driving four miles west, back to Old Lower Grange, because — who knows? — there might still be gas there, and if he really floored it, we might be able to make it out before the mayor flipped the lever and drowned us all.

"It was quite the drama," he always said. "Eh, Cass?"

And what was I supposed to say to that?

Because even though it was a good story, even though it was a story about me, it was also a story I had no way of remembering and really, technically, wasn't even there for.

So I didn't say anything. I sat at the table and let the stories wash over me — all the *Remember when?* and *Oh, that was so . . . !* and *I couldn't believe it when you . . . !*

And when Hannah burst out with "Oh, my God, remember when you threw mashed potatoes at me, Elijah? You were such a little brat," and everyone turned to stare at the wall behind my head, I lowered my face over my hot chocolate and blew down onto the surface, hiding myself in the billowing clouds of steam.

Thirteen

The next morning, everyone went to work — Hannah to the town hall, Elijah and Dad in the studio, and Mom back to school to clean up for the year.

And I went for a swim. With Liam.

When I got to the lake, he was already there. He had hauled the raft out from behind the tree and was leaning over it, pulling the broken bits off and tying fresh branches on with new string.

"I thought I could take it out," he said. "Stop you from drowning and all that. We could go out to the tree." He motioned to a paddle lying on the ground nearby. "See? I came prepared."

I knelt down next to him. "Do you think this'll hold both of us?"

He shrugged. "Only one way to find out. Remember, if we start sinking, just float and wave."

I couldn't bring myself to return his smile. Kneeling down like this, I could feel a knot in my leg — not pain, exactly, but a lingering tightness — and when I looked out at the water, my throat felt suddenly dry.

I wasn't quite ready to laugh about it yet.

Liam tied off a length of string in a complicated knot. "So what do you think?"

"Yeah, okay."

"Right. You take that end."

Together, we pushed and pulled the raft down the bank into the water. Liam climbed on, then shook his head when I tried to do the same.

"Swim first."

"What?"

"Your six, right?"

"Yeah, but that's much farther than —"

"You made it yesterday. And I'll stay close. If you want to stop, you can climb on." He dug the paddle in and pushed off the bottom, and then, with a few quick strokes, was out and away.

There was nothing I could do but kick off and follow.

Liam did stay close, so close he whacked me with the paddle twice and almost ran me over once. Which may have been deliberate, although he denied it. But even with the bruises, it was better with someone there. In a strange way, knowing I could stop and get a lift made me feel less like I needed one.

When we got there, Liam climbed off onto the platform and tethered the raft to the tree with some extra string.

He was grinning. "Wow! It *is* the fire tree."

"Didn't I say that?"

"Yeah, I know. It's just . . . it really is." He knelt down and peered through the gap in the platform. "You can see the pegs! Five, six, seven . . . cool!" He looked up at me. "Hey, do you think we could go down?"

"I don't know," I began, then stopped.

I had been thinking about it last night. About how silly it was, really. It was the fire tree. It was huge. It used to take Elijah ten minutes to get down with the bucket. Holding our breath, we'd never get anywhere near the town. And even if we did, it was dark down there. It wasn't like we'd be able to see anything. A lookout underwater wasn't a lookout anymore. It was . . . just an old, dead tree, I guess.

"What?"

Liam was staring at me. It was funny when you realized that none of the thoughts running through your head had made it into the outside world, that they were yours and yours alone.

Sometimes, given the kind of thoughts that ran through my head, it was a relief.

"It's high," I said finally. "I mean deep. It's —"

"Two hundred feet. I know. I made it, remember?" He made a snipping movement with his hands. "I didn't mean the whole way. Hang on."

Before I could stop him, he had stepped through the opening. Then he grinned, ducked his head under the water, and was gone.

I pulled myself past the raft and up onto the platform, then peered down into the opening. I could see his feet kicking and the edges of his shorts flapping around in the water. A steady stream of bubbles rose after him toward the surface.

Then his shorts were gone and his feet. The water

healed over him, and the stream of bubbles grew thinner and thinner until there was just dark and the surface was still and quiet, as if he had never been there.

It couldn't have been long. I knew because I've timed myself, and thirty-two seconds is my absolute limit before I get to the edge of my breath and lift my head, spluttering and wheezing.

I probably should have timed Liam. At least then I would have known when to start worrying. I would have known when to start tapping my fingers and rocking on my heels and scanning for bubbles. And maybe I wouldn't have finally freaked out and stuck my face in the water at the exact moment he was rocketing up through it like he'd been shot out of a cannon.

I reeled backward. "I think you've broken my nose."

He didn't reply. He was too busy spluttering and wheezing.

But he was also grinning.

"I think I went too far," he said finally. "You have to remember about getting back."

"Yeah."

"The pegs are good," he said. "You can pull yourself

down. Can't see much, though." He squinted out across the water. "So, the town square would be that way."

I thought back to my mosaic map from the day before. "I think so. And then the Old Lenton Road goes up around there." I pointed around the lake to where Elijah and I had stood all those years ago.

"I know," Liam replied. "Dad showed me."

"What, when you used to come up here? Could you see something?"

Liam climbed up onto the platform and sat down on the edge, dangling his feet over the side. "No, just in photos and stuff. He used to talk about it all the time. He had maps and everything. He used to go over them, like this." He made a scanning motion with one finger. "Mom made him get rid of it all. She said it wasn't good for him."

"How come?"

He shrugged. "There was this doctor in the city. He said Dad was trying to go back to the accident, to work something out. He said our brains do that — try to fix things, even when there's nothing to be fixed. He said Dad had to move on, do new things."

"Like the stuff he does for the town council?"

Liam nodded. "That's been good. Mom wasn't sure at first. But Finkle said to give it a go, see how things went."

"Finkle?"

"Yeah, it was his idea. He said the community should take care of people." Liam trailed one foot down into the water. "It's hard for Dad. One minute he can be fine and then . . ."

"Yeah." It wasn't a reply, but it was all I could think of to say.

"That thing the other day . . ." he began. He stopped, hesitated, as if making up his mind about something.

"What?"

"It wasn't your dad's pot." He looked up at me. "I mean it was, just not . . . It was the color."

"The color?" I frowned.

His eyes met mine briefly, then he spoke again, as if, having decided to talk, it was easier just to keep going. "Dad doesn't like red. Sometimes he's okay, and sometimes he flips out, starts shaking and stuff. We don't even wear red," he said. "Mom and I. Just in case. There was this one time . . ." He trailed off and made circles with his toe in the water's surface.

"Maybe . . . do you think it was the fire?" I said.

He stared at me.

"Sorry," I began. "If you don't want to —"

"Nah, it's not that." He shrugged. "It's not as if I remember it." He reached down and pulled a long splinter of wood from the side of the platform. "I don't think it was that. Fire isn't really red, anyway. It's orange and yellow and a whole mix of things."

I nodded. He was right. Things can trick you like that. People tell you fire is red, so that's what you see. But when you really look with your own eyes, it's completely different.

"The doctor figured it could have been anything," Liam went on. "Just some detail his brain got stuck on. He said it probably doesn't mean anything, even if it feels like it should."

As he spoke, I noticed he was rubbing the side of his leg, along the scar line.

"Does it hurt?" I asked.

"What, this?" He pulled the edge of his shorts up a little to reveal the edge of the knobbly scar. "I dunno. They said it can't. The nerves are dead or disconnected or something." He pressed the center of the scar with his finger, making it turn ghostly white. "But it's not their leg, is it?" He stood up suddenly. "You going to go down?"

I stared into the water, then shook my head. Maybe another day I would do it, pull myself slowly peg by peg into the darkness. Just not today.

"Okay." He started untying the raft. "You can ride this time."

I grabbed the paddle from where he'd leaned it against the tree. "Your turn to swim, then."

Liam raised his eyebrows.

"What, can't you make it?"

He grinned. "The real question is — can you steer that thing?" He took two steps across the platform and launched into a dive. Then he was off, striking out toward the shoreline in long, easy strokes.

When I finally made it back, after spinning and zigzagging halfway across the lake and back again, he was sitting on the bank, waiting.

I stood up and jumped off into the shallows. Or at least, that's what I meant to do.

What I actually did was stand up, wobble, and overbalance, then fall into the not-so-shallows.

I wasn't quite as close to shore as I'd thought.

When I surfaced, mud under my fingernails, a strand of lake weed draped in my hair like a braid, Liam was doing a slow clap. "Not bad," he called out. "Bit rough on the entry. I'd say yesterday's was more dramatic."

"Yeah." I grabbed the edge of the raft and towed it in toward him. "Remind me to work on that."

I guess I was ready to laugh about it now.

I pulled the raft through the shallows, and Liam came down to the edge to meet me. I was about to pass it to him when I stopped.

"Hang on."

"What?"

"Something's weird," I said. "Something's . . ."

I looked down into the water, through the water, to my feet. I wasn't staggering, the way I usually did near the edge. I wasn't trudging through the mud.

Because the mud wasn't thick here. Because there was something else underneath it, something my feet were touching and walking on, finding a firm, stable footing.

"There's a road," I said.

Liam knelt down. He was at the very edge, where mud met dry dirt and gravel. He used a stick to clear away the dirt along the line I was following. It was gray and faded. It had been weathered and washed out, and no one had walked on it in years. But it was regular, tightly packed, a sheet of once-dark stones flattened into place by long-ago hands.

Liam looked up at me. "Yeah," he said. "There is."

Fourteen

We didn't make plans for the next day or the day after that.

We didn't make any plans at all. We just turned up.

Sometimes I got there first, and sometimes Liam did. When I saw his bike parked alongside the break in the fence, I caught myself smiling.

I wondered if he did the same.

When we went out to the tree, we took turns on the raft — me swimming one way and Liam the other. He didn't need to stay alongside me anymore, though. I was getting stronger. I was coughing and spluttering less.

And I was getting faster. Even without flags and black lines, I could tell. The platform seemed closer, and not only because the shoreline was continuing to recede.

I still couldn't come close to Liam. When we swam next to each other, he pulled away from me immediately.

When I asked how he made it seem so easy, he shrugged. "It's all underwater."

That's why good swimmers look so relaxed, he said. You can't believe they're going that fast because it's all invisible. Everything that matters happens out of sight, under the surface. I nodded, thinking of Amber and her clean, butter-slice stroke.

Christmas came and went, and there were days when I couldn't get up there. There were days when Mom said we should spend time as a family, and we went to the pool, where Mom got mad because I wouldn't wear the rainbow-striped bikini she had bought me for Christmas. Or around to the Point, where I swam out past the Jet Skis till Mom started yelling and waving her arms, where I stared out across the surface, wondering if Liam was over there on the other side, hauling himself down.

Liam and I cleared off the road, at least as much as

we could. As you went farther up the bank, it veered off into the bush, where undergrowth and trees had grown up and over it.

We walked down the road toward the lake, into the water, but we kept bobbing up to the surface. I told Liam about my idea, of putting stones in my pockets, and he laughed.

We tried swimming down the road, following it as far as we could underwater. It was tricky, though. It was hard to stay down without anything to hang on to and difficult to stay with the line of the road when it was dark down there and everything was covered with mud.

Slowly, but noticeably now that we were paying attention, the water level continued to drop. We had to walk farther to get to the water. We made it farther down the road. We wondered how close we were — to the town, to the houses, to the places where our families used to live.

Out at the platform, we pulled ourselves down the pegs. The water got lower and lower. We dived farther and farther, counting ourselves down.

When Liam went under, I timed him so I'd know

when to panic. After a while, I stopped worrying. The bubbles always came back up. He was always there eventually, sticking his head through the opening, flicking his wet hair out of his eyes.

The water had receded below the level of the platform now, and the raft was tethered to a branch underneath us. We had to climb up to the platform using the pegs, the way people used to. It was weird to think that Elijah had been here, had done this before me, years and years ago.

One afternoon we sketched out a map in the mud halfway up the bank. Together we laid out the whole town, etching out its squares and sloping curves with pointed sticks.

Maybe it didn't make sense to draw a map in the mud when we could have just used paper, but it seemed right somehow. When it rained, it would be gone, washed away, but for now the sun baked it hard into the ground, solidifying the lines we had scratched out.

That was the day we found it.

I had pushed myself down from the edge of the raft, enjoying the feeling of spearing through the water, then kicking up toward the dark square that hung above me, framed against the brightness of the day. The sun was overhead, and it was light in the water. Even several feet down, I could see my hands in front of my face, watch my feet below me disappearing into the deep.

It was a fish, I thought at first when my toe brushed the edge of something. There was lake weed in closer to the shore, but you wouldn't get that this deep. But it hadn't felt like a fish. It hadn't felt like something that was passing, something I could nudge gently with my foot, sending it on its way through the water.

It had felt solid. It had felt . . . *there*.

When I surfaced, Liam was leaning down over the side of the raft. "What?" he asked.

"There's something down there."

"In the water? Like what?"

"Good question."

"Hang on. Do you think . . . ?"

"Only one way to find out."

We dived down.

We dived down together and freaked out bumping into each other in the shifting light. We surfaced together and freaked out when we realized the raft had drifted while we were under. Liam swam to get it while I stayed behind, treading water. After that we took turns, one of us staying with the raft, one of us slicing down into the lake.

I went feet first, tin-soldiering myself off the edge of the raft, pointing my toes down and down, straining for the tiny tip of whatever it was, if it had even been anything at all.

Liam went headfirst, hurling himself off the side. "It's safe," he said. "There's nothing shallow here. And we can use our arms better that way, to pull ourselves down."

I knew he was right, but I couldn't make myself do it. There was something about having my face lead the way into the dark that gave me the creeps.

"I'm going pretty deep," I said.

"I'm going deeper," Liam replied.

"I don't know," I said when he surfaced for what must have been the twentieth time. "Maybe it was nothing. Maybe . . ."

Then I stopped. Because Liam was grinning. Because there was something in his hand, clenched tightly between his fingers.

"You wouldn't have gotten that off with your toes," he said.

"What is it?"

"Wood."

"Oh." Something like disappointment washed over me. Wood. That was all. A submerged tree, maybe.

Liam shook his head. "Here."

Something else started growing in me then, something that wasn't disappointment but more like . . . anticipation, expectation. Because it wasn't that kind of wood. Not some bit of a stick or sheet of bark Liam had peeled off a tree, but part of a plank of wood, with milled edges and nail holes and the faint stain of rust.

Liam pulled himself up onto the raft. "There's more of it. A lot. Like a wall or something."

I laid the plank down on the raft and stared at it. How deep had it been? How old was it? And what was it from? What had it been part of, once upon a long time ago? The bakery, maybe? Or Tucker's? The old artists' studio! That was a wooden building.

Liam shook his head. "Not out here."

I looked around us. He was right. We were nowhere

near the town. We were on the other side, out in the hills. That meant the ground was closer to the surface of the water and more likely to be accidentally kickable by a foot, but also that there was nothing but trees and farms. Not even any houses, because they were all clustered down near the road so they could connect to the water and the power and all of that.

Liam went down again. He dived over and over, pulling up piece after piece of old, rotting wood and laying them out on the raft.

I stared at them, as if they were part of a puzzle we could fit together, as if they would tell me something if I just listened hard enough.

What I heard was Liam, bursting through the surface, spurting water through his teeth like a whale through its blowhole.

And then something else.

Someone yelling. A voice, calling out. "Hey!"

There was someone—a man—picking his way along the water's edge, one hand shading the sun from his face as he stared out across the lake.

Toward the raft.

Toward us.

I strained forward into the sunlight. For a second I felt hopeful. Maybe it was Elijah. He knew the way. And he suspected something the other week; I could see it in his face.

"Hey!" the voice repeated. "You kids!"

And it was a familiar voice now. It was a voice I'd heard at Sports Days and ceremonies and most recently in my own classroom.

It was Finkle.

Fifteen

"What are you kids doing here?"

As we approached the shore, Finkle came down to
the water's edge.

The mayor's face was dark. "There's no swimming
here!" he yelled. "There's no . . . Oh, it's you." His voice
softened suddenly.

At first, I thought he meant me. Dad was doing his
head, after all. He had come to my house.

But it was Liam he was talking to. And he
didn't sound angry anymore. He sounded friendly,
concerned.

"You all right there?" he asked as Liam waded
through the shallows, hauling the raft behind him.
"Need a hand?"

I stared at Finkle. What was he going to do—roll up his trousers and walk into the mud?

Liam shook his head. "I'm fine."

"You shouldn't be here. There's no swimming on this side."

Liam nodded. "Sorry."

Finkle frowned. "How did you get in here?"

I shot Liam a look, hoping he would keep quiet. Finkle must have driven up the old road and come in the gate. If anyone had a key, it would be him. If anyone was authorized, it would be him.

If anyone was trespassing, it would be us.

But Finkle wouldn't have seen the break in the fence. That was farther along. And our bikes were in the bushes on this side. Not hidden, exactly, but not obvious, either, unless you walked right by there, which you would never do if you were an authorized person coming through an officially approved gate.

I thought fast. I remembered how Elijah and I had picked our way along the shoreline all those years ago.

"We came around from the Point."

Finkle nodded at the raft. "On that? That's quite a distance."

"Yeah."

"Well, you shouldn't have," he said. "It's dangerous here. There are lots of snags on this side — submerged trees, sandbanks, that kind of thing."

Out of the corner of my eye, I saw Liam raise his eyebrows slightly. It made no sense, what Finkle had said, not if you knew anything about Old Lower Grange. If anything, there was more bush over on the other side, near the Point. This side was slightly clearer, being closer to the town itself. It was true that there were some hills, but there were hills everywhere, and they weren't the same thing as sandbanks at the beach that would rise up suddenly and break your unsuspecting neck.

Finkle shaded his face as he looked out across the water. "What is that, anyway?" He pointed toward the tree.

"I think it's the fire tree." I followed his gaze. "But it's not dangerous or anything. It's just —"

"The fire tree?" Finkle took a few steps closer to the edge, craning forward. "Above the water?"

"Yeah," Liam replied, "you can see the pegs and everything."

"But that's . . ." Finkle blinked. He lowered his hand from his face and peered down at the hardened mud at our feet. "I had no idea it was this low." Something came across his face. "This isn't good at all."

For a moment he was lost in thought, then he looked up quickly, as if he'd suddenly remembered we were there. "Well, what are you two going to do? You can't stay here. I can give you a lift back to town if you want. Unless someone's waiting for you at the Point?"

Liam turned his head at the same time I did, in the direction of the hole in the fence. Then we both stopped. The bikes could wait.

"Mom was coming back later," I said. "But I can tell her not to bother."

"All right, then. Come on."

We followed Finkle back through the trees, through the gate to where he'd parked his silver truck. Behind us, Finkle ran the chain back through the wire and snapped the lock shut, then rattled it firmly to make sure it was secure.

As we bumped our way along the dirt road back to town, he kept up a steady stream of talk. About how low the water was: he knew it had been dry, he said, but he hadn't expected it to be so bad.

"I like to come up every now and then," he said. "Keep an eye on things. It's all on the computer, of course." He waved a hand in the direction of the river, up toward the power station. "I could leave it up to the engineers. But there are some things you can only see with your own eyes — trees sticking out of the water, kids putting themselves at risk." He gave us a meaningful look in the rearview mirror. "I like to do a job myself. In the end, I'm the mayor. It's my name out there, my face. Well, my whole head, really." He smiled broadly at me. "How's your father doing with that?"

"I'm not sure," I said. "He doesn't really show us stuff while he's working on it."

"Well, he'd better make me look good." He laughed. Then he flicked his eyes across to where Liam was sitting. "Speaking of fathers . . ."

Liam nodded, as if he had expected this.

"How's he doing? Enjoying the work?"

"Yeah, it's been good."

"It has, hasn't it?" Finkle said enthusiastically.

"I thought so, too. I mean, he really seems okay, doesn't he?"

Liam flushed a little, then replied. "Yeah, it suits him. He says he likes the weeding best."

"And what about you? Everything okay? Enjoy the camp, did you?"

"Um, yeah. It was great. Thanks."

I frowned. It could only be our school camp that Finkle was talking about, but then why didn't he ask me as well? And why was Liam thanking him? I tried to catch Liam's eye, but he had looked away and was staring out the window.

We stopped at the bottom of the hill so Finkle could unlock the barrier, then eased out onto the main road. The smooth surface was a relief after the ridges of the dirt road and the way we had been careering wildly around the sharp turns.

We picked up speed for the short stretch of road until we came to the outskirts of town, then Finkle jabbed at the brake to slow us back down. We rolled past the school and the timber yard, then around the corner onto Main Street. As the town square came into view, Finkle flicked another glance at us in the rearview mirror.

"I'll see you both at the centenary, I hope? Not long now."

I nodded. I was only too aware of how close the centenary celebrations were, what with Hannah constantly stressing about the book, and Dad doing the same over the head and how to make Finkle look good while still maintaining his artistic integrity.

"Well, shall I let you out here somewhere?"

Finkle slowed to a stop, and Liam opened the door on his side. "Thanks," he began, but then the truck jerked forward. Finkle was staring out the window to the left, at the clock tower.

"Maybe a bit farther?" he said suddenly. "Maybe just up here? Should we —?"

Liam yanked the door shut as the truck lurched forward past the square and into the intersection. A horn blared behind us.

"What are you doing?" A car swerved around us on the right-hand side, its driver yelling angrily out the window. "I thought you were parking!"

"Sorry!" Finkle called. "My fault. Changed my

mind." He swiveled in his seat. "Sorry. Just thought I'd take you a bit farther."

"Just drop us off at the town hall," Liam said. "You're going there, anyway. And I can check on Dad."

"Of course! Good idea." Finkle sounded relieved as he kicked the truck back into gear and cruised up the hill.

When we had parked outside his office, he turned back toward us. "Remember what I said before. It's not safe where you were. Technically, I could have you prosecuted. Don't let me catch you up there again, okay?"

I stifled a smile as I climbed out of the truck, then hurried around to Liam's side. I wanted to remind him how *technically* not being caught wasn't the same as not going.

But Liam didn't look my way. He followed Finkle inside, and the heavy door closed shut behind them with a sigh.

Sixteen

"I didn't know if you'd come back," I said as Liam pulled alongside the raft. I had seen him coming through the trees and down the bank. I had watched his long, relaxed stroke as he made his way to me across the water.

It wasn't Liam I'd been keeping an eye out for. It was Finkle. Or any other so-called authorized person who might try to tell us we had to move on.

I even had my excuse all ready — that I had just come to get the raft, that I was heading straight back to the Point. Sure, I had been stopped in one spot for about half an hour, but everyone knew Cassie Romano had weak lungs. Everyone knew she had to pace herself.

Sometimes living in a small town could work to your advantage.

It didn't make sense if you knew that my bike was up here, that I'd had to trek all the way up here on foot, and that paddling over to the Point would mean leaving it behind again.

But there was no way for anyone to know that.

No one except Liam.

He threw an arm up onto the side of the raft and swung one leg over. I shifted my weight to the other end as a counterbalance while he clambered up.

He stretched out next to me on the warm wood. "Did you think I was going to let Finkle scare me off? He's all talk."

I raised my eyebrows. "Yeah, you seem pretty friendly with him. Or he's pretty friendly with you. Or something. How come he was asking about camp?"

Liam looked as if he wished he had a leaf to strip, but they were hard to come by in the middle of the lake. "I'm not really supposed to tell anyone. I mean, I don't care, but he said not to make a big thing out of it."

"Out of what?"

"The scholarship. At least that's what he called it. For the fees."

"The town council paid your camp fees?"

"Yeah. Or no. I'm not sure. I think he might have paid it himself. Mom said we couldn't afford it. I don't know if Dad mentioned it at work or something, but the next thing we know, Finkle's on the phone offering to pay for the whole thing."

"Wow. That's pretty nice of him."

"Yeah, I know."

Our camp was a big deal. It wasn't some overnight pitch-a-tent-in-the-bush-and-cook-your-own-bread trip. It was a train all the way up to the city, two nights in a hotel, surfing lessons, and a bus tour. It was expensive. Mom made me do chores for months to help pay mine off.

Liam raised his arms in a big, lazy stretch. "It's so cool up here. We should tell the others."

I felt myself stiffen. "It's cool because it's just us," I said. "Don't you think?"

"Maybe just a few?" He turned toward me slightly. "Maybe just —?"

I shook my head. "I don't want to."

How many was a few, anyway? Even if we only told Emily and Max and Amber, that would already be too many. That would already be splashing and squealing and the kind of loud messing around that left no room for scratching maps out of mud or trailing your toes lazily off a raft or sitting quietly with your back to the warm wood of a drowned tree.

I had always been the girl who focused quietly on the spine of a leaf while other kids ran around squealing. And Liam had always been the boy who looked up when someone came along, who stood up and walked off easily with them, smiling and talking.

Sometimes I wondered if it was because I spent the first couple of months of my life alone in a plastic box that I got used to being by myself, *with* myself. But Liam was born with a ready-made friend. So he learned to be with people, to make room for them in his space. And then all of a sudden he didn't need to, because it was just him.

"Do you miss him?" I said. And then I froze. Because that was one of those thoughts that should have happened only in my head, and now there it was, hanging out in the still summer air.

"Miss who?"

I scrambled for something to say. His dad? Could I pretend that's who I meant? Liam often talked about him when we sat out here like this, together but apart, looking out at the water and not at each other. Somewhere along the way that had become possible out here, but when we stood up to head back, we pretended it didn't exist anymore, that those conversations had happened somewhere else, to other people.

But that didn't make sense this time. His dad wasn't gone. He was just . . . different.

Liam's head turned slightly. "You mean Luke."

"Luke?"

"My brother."

I nodded. Yes. That's who I meant.

"It feels weird to say his name."

It felt weird to hear it. Everyone knew what had happened, of course. Everyone knew there was a *miracle baby* and another one who wasn't so lucky.

"No one ever says it." There was a tightness in Liam's

voice. "Like he didn't live long enough to make it stick or something, like he wasn't an actual person."

"That's not . . ." I began. "I mean, I just forgot—that's all."

"Yeah." Liam drew his knees in to his chest and wrapped his arms around them. His knuckles clenched pale across the tan of his legs. "I know."

We fell silent, but it wasn't a comfortable silence. It was the kind of silence where it feels like time is stretching and stretching, and if you don't let the pressure off, something will snap.

"Sorry," I said finally. "I shouldn't have asked that. You don't have to talk about it. I mean, I know—"

"No, you don't," Liam said quietly. "You don't know. People think they do, but they don't." As he spoke, the thumb of one hand ran roughly over and over the edge of his scar, turning it briefly white with each kneading movement. "I bet you didn't know he was the good one," he said. "Mom said so. I was always crying, and he was always calm. She said there was something in his eyes, like he was an old soul."

"She said that to you?"

He shook his head. "It was in one of those baby

books. She was writing everything down. Every time we burped and slept and cried. It's all there, for five weeks. Then . . ."

I nodded. There was no need to say anything to fill in that gap.

"You know how there's always one twin?" Liam went on. "One who takes more, who gets stronger, and one who hangs on and takes what's left." His voice took on a lightness that didn't quite ring true, as if he was delivering a punch line he didn't find funny. "So that's me. The one who hangs on. Parents say they don't have favorites, but he was hers already, and we were hardly even born." He stood up suddenly and leaned out across the metal frame that surrounded the platform. "I always wondered if it was me . . . if I caused it."

My head snapped up. He couldn't mean what I thought he meant. That didn't make any sense.

"He was the good one," Liam repeated. "I was always crying. Screaming, Mom said. All the time. Like *all the time.*" He gouged a piece of rotting wood off the raft and crumbled it between his fingers. "She said car trips were horrible, that she was always turning around to settle me." His voice cracked a little, coming out finally in a whisper. "I guess that's okay when someone else is driving."

"Liam . . ." I began, then trailed off. He was shaking his head.

"Dad was on his own with us. What if he was turning around? Because I was screaming. And then . . ."

"No," I said quickly.

"Why not?" He glanced down at me briefly, then back out across the water. "There was no reason for it. Straight road. Good weather. Clear visibility. That's what they said."

"You can't think like that. No one knows what happened, not really." As I spoke, headlines unrolled themselves before my eyes. "Driver Error: Fatigue a Factor?"

"Yeah." Liam let the crumbled pieces fall slowly through his fingers down onto the water. "But they think they do."

He was right. People thought they knew stuff. They thought that what mattered was what they could see. They let what was on the surface tell the story.

I should have known better. I did know better. I knew that a heavy red glaze could cover a network of tiny hairline fractures that would shatter something utterly if you struck it hard enough in just the right spot. I knew that if you could bring yourself to stop staring at the smooth, clean surface and push your way through it, you might be surprised at the world buried deep underneath.

"You're right," Liam said suddenly.

"About what?"

"This." He nodded out across the lake. "Let's not tell anyone. Let's just keep it for ourselves."

"Yeah." I smiled slightly, glad of the chance to talk about something simpler, to hear that easy lightness return to his voice. "Let's."

"And also," he said, standing up suddenly, wobbling the raft so that I had to hang on to the sides to stop myself from tumbling off, "let's find this thing."

Seventeen

Liam had been clever yesterday.

While I was worrying about being prosecuted, he was counting his strokes. He was positioning the raft on the bank, pointing it in the direction we needed to go to get back to the spot.

"Good thinking," I said, looking up at him from where I sat on the still-wobbling wood.

"I counted 297 to here," he said. "Yesterday we were at 312. Give or take."

We went out a little farther—Liam swimming, counting his strokes, and me following on the raft.

We dived down. Both of us. We had goggles and flippers, which I had stuffed into my backpack and lugged up the hill. And we had a flashlight.

Liam raised his eyebrows. "What's that for?"

"What do you think?" I pressed the rubber button on the shaft and flashed the light on and off.

"Underwater?" He snorted. "That'll last about ten seconds."

He was wrong. It lasted five. Approximately. Not that I was counting. It had taken me long enough to fix it to my head using the Velcro strap I had brought specially. It made me feel like an underwater explorer, the kind you see on Discovery Channel documentaries hauling themselves through underground caves on their way to discover treasure and fantastical lands. And, in my case, to discover the fact that batteries and water don't play well together.

When I came back up, Liam was laughing. "You realize they have waterproof flashlights, don't you?"

"I do now."

"Forget the flashlight," he said. "We'll just feel around until we find it."

We were close enough. Close enough to find whatever it was quickly with the goggles and the pair of flippers we had to share between us and the mostly useless flashlight. The goggles weren't very useful, either, not once you got a few feet down, but they did help me feel better. Having something on my face, protecting my eyes, made going down headfirst slightly less creepy.

We took turns. We dived. We kept an eye out for Finkle — for anyone.

We brought up pieces of wood and pieces of wood and . . . more pieces of wood.

"It's a shed," Liam said finally, surfacing for what felt like the hundredth time.

"A shed?" Of course. That would be it. An old wooden shed, left to rot out on someone's property.

On the one hand, I felt a bit let down.

A shed wouldn't have any rooms to explore. It wouldn't have passages to lead you down, nooks and crannies to uncover. A shed wouldn't have much of anything. It would just be a space, a present you open to find an empty box.

But, on the other hand, I couldn't help feeling a bit excited. When someone gives you a present, you can't help unwrapping it, can you? You can't help opening it up, just in case.

"The door's on the other side," Liam said. "It's got a padlock."

"Locked?"

"I think so. Or rusted shut."

When I went down, I realized that he was right. It was definitely locked, the padlock snapped tight through the links of a thick chain. I tried rattling the door, but although it was loose, the hinges were still bonded to the metal frame.

"We need a hammer," I said.

Liam laughed. "A special *underwater* hammer? You could strap it to your head."

"Ha, ha." I thought about the door, the hinges. "Or not a hammer. A screwdriver."

Liam shook his head. "The screws would be rusted."

"Well, what, then? We want to get the door open, don't we? It's stuck. So we need something to open it with."

I picked up a piece of wood and held it in the palm of my hand. *The solid weight of history and all that.* It was surprisingly light. And crumbly.

Something flashed across Liam's face.

"What?"

He raised a hand and smacked himself across the forehead. "We're such idiots." He stared at me. "Actually, a hammer would be kind of helpful. Here . . ." He reached out a hand. "Give me the flashlight."

"Oh, now you want —"

I didn't get the chance to finish. He grabbed the flashlight, strap and all, and said, "Wish me luck!" Then he sucked in a big breath of air and was gone.

Gone. Under. He was gone and he was under, and he had been both things before, but this time was different. This time he wanted a hammer but took a flashlight, and I didn't know what he was going to do, only that he was gone too long.

That he was under too long.

Probably. Not that I was counting or anything.

I leaned over the edge of the raft, scanning the surface for signs. For bubbles, a rush of something, anything.

Nothing.

Even though I wasn't counting, it had to be more than thirty, definitely. More than forty. Fifty, maybe. Was that even possible? There were people who did that, who held their breath for ages. I had seen them on documentaries, hauling themselves down long cables that led them, like ladders, deep into the ocean. Maybe they had flashlights strapped to their heads. Or maybe I was mixing them up with the cavers. But the flashlights didn't matter, probably. It was the breath that mattered. Wasn't it always the breath? And they trained for it, didn't they, for days and weeks and months and years? They didn't just grin and grab a flashlight and take off for . . . how long now? A minute?

I should have counted properly. It was so easy to speed up without realizing, to tell yourself it was a minute when really it was only thirty or maybe forty seconds.

I should have done *one-cat-and-dog, two-cat-and-dog, three* . . .

That way I would have known how long it was.

Too long.

There were no bubbles, no churn.

Panic stabbed at my chest.

I had to go down, but could I make it — without flippers to kick myself down, to get to the shed?

To get to Liam.

I took a deep breath.

Wish me luck.

Something slammed up from underneath me, tumbling me off the raft and into the water.

A head, hands, a boy. Coughing and spluttering and grabbing at the air.

"Cassie! Ow!"

"Ow yourself!"

We hung there, treading water. I listened to his breathing, rattled and rough.

"Are you okay?"

He nodded, then pulled himself slowly over to the raft. "Yeah. I . . . hang on." He held on to the side for a minute until his breathing slowed.

"Where were you?" I said.

He grinned. "I got in."

"You got it open?"

"Not exactly. I mean, yeah, but . . . not the way you think."

He explained.

How we were idiots. Because as soon as we found a door, that was all we could think about. Because doors were the way into a place. Even though we'd already broken off a big chunk of roof, making it weak, making a hole. Which Liam could hammer through, with an otherwise-useless flashlight, and then pull himself through, and past, and down into the shed.

Where there was a big space of nothing he could swim down and into and feel his way around, running slowly out of air and then, just before he gave up and kicked his way back through the hole, finding it.

"What?"

Liam grinned. He held up his other hand, which had been sculling underwater, and I saw that he was holding something.

Something fat and roundish, made of plastic and glass.

A side-view mirror?

Or at least part of one. The housing had broken down, and it was cracked and split.

But you could still see what it was, what it had once been — the cloudy glass panel, the faded splinters of red plastic.

I stared at him. "There's a *car* down there?"

"Yep."

My mind raced with possibilities. A car? Drowned in the flood?

I thought about Dad in the Valiant, panicking about gas. Thinking for a brief, crazy moment about racing back into Old Lower Grange.

And then I shivered.

What if someone did get caught in the flood?

What if there was someone in there — a body?

A skeleton by now.

Liam laughed. "Nah, it'll just be some old clunker someone left behind. Pretty cool, still . . . huh?" He broke off.

"What?" I began. Then I felt it. The water moving beneath us — only slightly, but it was there. Bubbles coming up.

"Is that you?" I said.

He shook his head. "I'm here. I'm —"

Then it popped up with a sickening bounce — something gray and sort of round and sort of . . .

I screamed.

It was a head, bobbing between us, a skull, slimy with lake weed.

"Oh, my God," I said. "Get it away, get it . . ."

We both scrambled backward at once. We were a mess of arms and legs and flippers, and the thing was sitting on the water's surface, grinning at us with its broken mouth and its lopsided eyes and . . .

Oh.

"It's okay," I said, because it was suddenly.

It was still weird — very weird, in fact — but it was okay.

I swam over and scooped it in to my chest, then kicked back and sat it up on the raft.

"Jeez," said Liam. "I thought it was a . . . you know."

"Yeah." I ran one finger along the ridge of an eye socket. "It kind of is."

He peered closer. "What is it, anyway?"

"A head," I said. "Clearly."

I told him about Dad's artistic vision.

He nodded slowly. "Right." Then he peered at the head. "It's pretty weird-looking. I guess it's been under there for a while."

"Yeah," I said. "But that's not the reason."

Then I grinned and climbed up onto the raft, and we headed back for shore.

Eighteen

"Where on earth did you get this?"

I almost didn't tell Dad about the head. I knew it would lead to questions I'd find hard to answer.

But I also knew it might lead to answers I wouldn't get any other way.

And I had to know. We had opened the box, and this had come out. This and a mirror, attached to a panel, attached to a car.

"The lake?" Dad said. "Did Elijah take you?"

"Not exactly," I began. "I . . . go there sometimes. It washed up."

It was kind of true.

Dad frowned. "Cass, you're not to swim up there on your own, all right?"

I nodded.

That was also true, these days.

"Washed up, did it? I guess I can't say I'm surprised. I had some firing problems back then . . . air bubbles, that sort of thing."

Dad peered at the head. I had let it dry in the sun, then wrapped it in my towel and carried it down in my backpack. The hair was a bit smudged, and there was a large crack at the base of the skull from when I'd jolted over a big rock, but otherwise it looked the same as when it emerged from the depths.

Completely unrecognizable.

Except to Dad, of course.

He snapped his fingers. "But that's . . . but it can't be!" He rubbed the back of his neck with one hand. "How bizarre."

"What?"

"I did leave some of these behind when we moved." Dad smiled, remembering. "I was learning back then, so they weren't very good, but mostly I just liked the idea of it — of them staying behind, 'living' in the town for us."

"That's . . . um, kind of creepy."

"That's one way of looking at it," Dad said. "As you know, I have a different vision. What's strange is that this wasn't one of them."

"One of what?"

"The heads I left behind." Dad went to the shelf where he kept his books and ran his finger along the spines. "Yes, here it is." He pulled out an old album and leafed through it. "See?"

There was a page of notes and sketches and a small, faded photo taped down the bottom, partly obscured by Dad's thumb.

Across the top, in thick black marker, was a single word:

FINKLE.

"Finkle?" I craned forward. "I didn't know you'd done him before. But that doesn't . . ."

Look much like him, I was going to say.

Even taking into account twelve years of water and the uniqueness of Dad's artistic vision, the head we'd found had nothing in common with Finkle. It was too small, for one thing, and the hair was all wrong, and the nose was —

"Not *that* Finkle," Dad said. "His wife."

"Finkle's wife let you do her head?"

"Of course! Well, I'm sure she would have if she'd known about it." Dad tapped the photo with one clay-brown finger. "I took this in the supermarket, from behind the bread display. Not hiding, exactly, just . . . Anyway, it was a gift for Finkle. He was going over to the Lenton Festival and said he'd drop some pots off at the Craft Market for me. This was my way of saying thanks."

I stared at the mangled head. "Right."

Dad looked thoughtful. "She left him not long after that, actually. Moved up to the city. I always wondered if the head had something to do with it." He grinned. "Not seriously, but —"

I cut him off. "So how did it end up in the lake?"

"That's what I can't work out. If I remember, it was a few months before they dammed the town. We were getting ready to move, packing everything up."

"But what about the head?"

"Well, that's what I'm saying. That's when I gave it to him." Dad stroked the smooth curve of the skull absently. "I packed it into a box and put it in the trunk of his car myself."

"And now it's in the lake," I said. "At least it was in the lake, and now it's here."

Dad brightened. "Yes, it's quite fitting, isn't it — like it's returned to the place of its birth. The circle of life and all that."

"Yeah, except that this isn't the place of its birth," I said. "In fact, it was closer to your old studio when it was up in the lake."

"Good point. Well, maybe that's why it was there. Maybe it was trying to get back home again."

"This isn't really helping," I said through clenched teeth.

"No, I suppose not. But it's interesting, isn't it?" Dad smiled. "I could ask Finkle if you like, when I see him next. Which reminds me . . ." He gestured toward a low table in the center of the room. There was something perched on it, something vaguely head-shaped, swathed in Bubble Wrap.

"Is that —?"

Dad nodded. "Just in time."

He was right about that. The centenary was only a few days away. "Shouldn't it be on, like, a stand or something?" I said.

"*Plinth* is the word you're after." Dad sighed. "And yes, it should. But Finkle insists I don't attach it until just before the ceremony. I think he's worried about bird poo or something."

Tires crunched outside, and I looked out to see Elijah's truck pulling up.

"Perfect timing!" Dad said. "I'll pack this thing properly and give it to him to take in tomorrow."

He slid Finkle's head into the box and closed the flaps over the top, then reached for the tape to seal them down tight.

Nineteen

When Dad told Mom about the head, she frowned.

That was probably because it was her usual response to anything to do with his heads.

Then she dropped her fork onto her plate with a clatter, sending flecks of spaghetti sauce flying.

That was probably because he had suddenly produced the head from under his chair and set it in the middle of the table, like a zombie centerpiece.

"Andrew! Get that thing out of here!"

"Don't talk about Mrs. Finkle like that," Dad teased. "She's a lovely lady. Was, anyway. It's been a long time. Anything could have happened, I suppose."

"Twelve years. Has it really been that long?" Mom sighed. "Where did you get this?"

"It . . . washed up, apparently. At the lake."

Dad told Mom about the day Finkle came over. How he'd put the head in his trunk. How he could see him now, clear as if it was yesterday, waving from his little red car as he sped off in a cloud of dust.

But he didn't tell Mom about me swimming.

Maybe that was because I'd been keeping his head-related secrets for years, telling Mom he was busy glazing pots when he was really obsessing over how to make someone's ear look slightly less like a deformed cabbage.

Maybe it was because it was hard for anyone who wasn't Hannah to say much of anything at dinner and afterward, and on into the rest of the evening, because she was so busy telling us all about the centenary preparations. About how the book was finished and the ceremony was all planned and the band was going to be significantly less lame this time, and she was feeling a bit nervous about everything, but she was sure it would be fine in the end, an *occasion to remember,* and no matter what anyone said she was proud of herself and so was Howard, because she had worked really hard and done an excellent job.

"See?" After the dishes were cleared away, she emptied her work satchel, set her laptop down between us, then laid a sheaf of papers out across the table. *Printing proofs,* she called them. She said she didn't have a proper copy yet, but nearly everything was here. "I just had to change a few things, fix a couple of typos." She turned to me. "You should thank me, Cass. They tried to call you Carrie at one point." She smoothed the pages down with the palms of her hands. "But basically this is it."

I leaned over as she flicked through the glossy, oversize pages.

It was amazing — almost like a real book. There were headlines and photos and text, all wrapping around one another at odd angles in a way that looked funky and interesting, as if it had been carefully designed by someone who knew what she was doing and was on top of everything, and not someone who at any point in her life would have become paralyzed, sobbing uncontrollably halfway up a tree.

It looked different from the way it had on the screen, on the computer. It looked polished and finished.

But it looked different for other reasons, too.

I turned to Hannah. "What happened to the stuff about the bushfire?" Six years ago a fire had come within a mile of the town. I had seen Hannah working on a page about it. She had laid it out with some photos and an interview with the Clancys, whose farm had been threatened.

Now it was just gone.

Hannah waved a hand. "Oh, I deleted that. I couldn't get it to fit properly in the end. Nothing really happened, anyway. And we could use the space. Howard wanted to put in more about tourism."

There were other stories missing, too, when I thought about it. The time the Porters' sheep got out and stopped traffic on the highway, making the news as far away as Perth. The year Miranda Hopkins made the top one hundred of *Australian Idol*. And the time Sam Farrington got lost in the bush, and half the town went out searching . . . No, that one was still there, but it had been reduced to a tiny square and added to the page about the endangered bilby, in a way that made them seem weirdly connected.

"Can I look on here?" I reached for the laptop.

Hannah nodded. I pulled it over in front of me

and snapped it open. It blinked quickly to life, and I clicked onto the "Town Council" folder that was sitting on the desktop. Inside that was another folder called "Centenary," then another called "Book," and inside that were row after row of documents.

Draft 1, Draft 2, Update, Revised Version, November 19, November 19.2, New Revision . . . the names scrolled on and on.

Hannah was right. She had done a lot of work. She had done all these drafts, all these versions. All of them telling the story, of the town. All of them telling the same story differently. She had deleted some things and added others. She had narrowed things down, and now she had these shiny pages that would soon be bound tightly together into a book, solid and final.

My fingers hovered above the keyboard.

It was a funny thing about computers. You could just press the delete key and make things disappear. It wasn't like a hard copy, where if you put Liquid Paper over something, you could scratch it off later and see what you had written, faint and ghostly but not gone; where even if you used pencil and rubbed something out, you could still see the marks, the thin patch on the paper that told you something different had come before it, that what you could see wasn't all there had ever been.

Computers were different. You could save the changes and pretend they never existed in the first place. They didn't leave a trail but made a smooth, slick surface that told you it was truth, had always been, would always be.

Is that what would happen? I wondered. Now that we had the centenary book, the official new story of Lower Grange, would that solidify into its own kind of truth? Would anyone ever bother to go back and see what sat quietly in the margins?

As Hannah talked on about the band and the plinth and the quality of locally made sausages, I clicked back out of the "Centenary" folder and back into "Town Council."

Then I noticed something.

There was a document open, sitting there minimized in the corner of the screen. I clicked in the top right-hand corner to close it, but a window popped up.

Save changes before closing?

I don't know, I thought.

They're not my changes.

It's not my document.

I clicked cancel, and the document popped up in front of me.

Meeting, January 11.

They were notes from a town council meeting two days earlier, Hannah's rapidly typed notes, full of errors she would clean up later.

EL: 12 Barker St. resident complains about neighbor dog. Regulations? Get someone out there to check it out. Refer to ranger.

GC: Sidewalks on Kitchener St. need work. can we sned someone to look asap plz.

AM: shd have gourmet sasuages for shindig NO MSG the health of our children is at stake (steak? ha!) and blahblahblah

HF: east side lake fence needs work, higher, stronger, maybe new fence between east side and Point as well, plus new signs and stuff, do something etc. VERY IMPORTANT to keep people out. VERY IMPORTANT, yes Howard we get it, we do!! maybe electrify fence!!! the safety of our children and all that. mild electric shocks no problem if prevent drowning. Refer: enginnering?

There was lots more — tightly packed lines about trash collection and fire roads and overdue rates — but this was where I stopped.

A new fence? Higher, stronger, *electrified*?

Wow. Finkle really meant it when he said he didn't want people up there.

I clicked behind the document, into the "Town Council" folder. There were more documents labeled "Meetings," going back years. They weren't all Hannah's. Most of them were from way before her time. I guess she just had them as a record, so she could look back and go, *HF said this in June 2005* or *12 Barker resident is only complaining about dog because neighbor wouldn't pay for new fence two years ago* or whatever.

There were two documents for each date — one full of messy notes, like Hannah's, and one labeled "Minutes." These were neat and formal. They'd had the mistakes and the *Yes, Howard!* comments deleted. Now they looked official and serious.

I scrolled back through the directory, through the documents, through the years. All the way back, twelve years ago, to when the town was drowned.

There was stuff about protests and debates and

arguments. There was stuff about levers and bands and sausages. There was stuff about swimming pools and lakes and fences.

Lots of stuff about lakes and fences.

Report suggests east side of lake for swimming area. Close to town, easy access for residents.

HF: concern about snags and danger.

RW: same on other side?

HF: west side better outlook, appeal for tourists

BT: residents should take priority over tourists!

HF: safety of our children. East side not an option.

AM: need to consider the recommendation of the report.

HF: need to consider the opinion of the mayor, who is your boss!

The discussion went on for several pages. No, several meetings. RW, BT, AM, and every other set of initials wanted the swimming area on the east, but HF pushed for the west. And kept pushing, until first RW, and then BT, and finally AM and everyone else either agreed or gave in.

And finally, the neat and formal, official and serious version of the minutes read simply:

It was resolved that the new swimming area would be established on the west side of the lake, with ample parking and an access road extending from the highway.

Moved: AM; Seconded: BT; all in favor.

I looked down at the table. Hannah had opened the printing proofs to a double-page spread of the lake. There were people swimming and picnicking and floating around on rubber rings. The walls of the dam rose up in the distance, and there was a smaller photograph inset of the viewing platform, where a family stood, pointing out across the water.

The photo didn't extend east. The edge of the water blurred as it reached the fancy border Hannah had made to look like bubbles flowing around the side of the page. There was no sign of the possibly future-electrified fence, of the padlock and the warning signs, of the uneven edges of what might have once been a road, of the lengths HF would go to, to keep people out.

But why? There weren't any snags, not really. The water was lower than it had ever been, and we'd never run into anything, at least not accidentally. To find anything, we'd had to dive down and down, holding our breath longer than I had thought humanly possible.

Even then, what we'd found wasn't exactly dangerous — a shed, a car, a weird Finkle head.

Come to think of it, it was kind of ironic that it was a Finkle head in the lake, when Finkle was the one who didn't want anyone swimming there.

"Hey!" Hannah reached across and pulled the laptop toward her. She snapped the screen shut. "I didn't say you could look at that stuff."

"There were unsaved changes," I said. "A window popped up. I was —"

"Oh, dammit," she said. "I hope I didn't lose anything. I've been so busy, I . . . never mind. I'll type them up later. I can probably remember everything if it comes to that." She slid the laptop back into its padded sleeve, then leaned out over the table and began rolling up the proofs. "The point is it's nearly done. I think it's going to be great!"

Around the table, everyone nodded and I joined in. But it wasn't so much that I was agreeing. It was more that I was thinking.

I was thinking about Hannah making up her

minutes from memory, about what she might forget or misremember — just slightly, just enough to make it GC who cares about the MSG rather than AM, and maybe that doesn't matter right now, but who knows? One day it might. Maybe one day a great wave of MSG-related illness would strike New Lower Grange, and AM would say, *Well, you know, I was always concerned about this,* and use his incredible foresight as a platform to run for mayor, and then someone would go back through the records and say, *Well, actually, no, that wasn't you as it turns out,* and before we knew it, Gladys Cropp would be leading our town and no one would be quite sure how it happened.

I was thinking about the way something can slide in so easily over the top of something else — a cleaner version, a neater account, a smooth glaze over a maze of hairline fractures, a delete key threading silence across incriminating paragraphs, five thousand swimming pools of water pouring onto an inconvenient town.

And before long no one remembers what was under there to begin with.

Before long, they have a hard time remembering there was ever anything there at all.

Twenty

That night, a dream pulled me from sleep.

It was about Atlantis. And puzzles. About pieces of wood and mosaic and my clumsy hands trying to click things together, but it was hard to see through the water and what with Finkle being everywhere — at school and the town hall and the lake and Dad's studio. And whenever I found a piece I thought might fit, whenever I was giving it just the exact right jiggle it needed to maybe, possibly slot itself into place, he would jump up, waving his hands, saying, *No, no, that can't go there. Look!*

And I would look down and wonder what I had been thinking because that wasn't the right piece, maybe not even the right puzzle.

I lay on my back and stared up at the ceiling. Around me, the curtains flapped in the breeze that whispered through the open window. Snatches of moonlight wobbled this way and that, throwing shadows up and down the walls.

I knew it was silly. But I couldn't help thinking that maybe it was something. Once I'd had the thought, I couldn't seem to let it go. The Finkle head, underwater. What was it doing in a shed, in the hills? Was it even in the shed? Or was it maybe just down there in the mud somewhere, and we disturbed it, with our diving and rattling of doors and breaking of wood.

Even if it was just in the mud, how did it get there, all the way outside of town, near a shed, near a car?

A red car.

Suddenly, a piece clicked. Red plastic flaking off the mirror. Dad waving good-bye to Finkle. Finkle driving off in his little red car. A little red car with his wife's head right there in the trunk, right there just waiting for the metal to rust and crumble so it could bob freakishly up and out of its watery grave and all the long way to the surface.

That was *Finkle's* car under there?

That made sense, didn't it? A kind of sense at least. It didn't explain why it was there, but maybe it was like Liam said. Maybe it was just an old clunker by then. Old clunkers were hard to sell. That's why you saw old cars slowly falling apart in people's front yards, rusted bodies dumped in pockets of bushland. That's why there was an abandoned-car hotline, a number you could call so someone would come with a tow truck and drag the ugly things away, out of sight, out of mind.

Maybe Finkle decided it was easier just to leave it in the shed.

I didn't ask myself why the head was still there, why he had left it in the trunk.

One look at it and that question answered itself.

Why would any man give that to his wife?

That was when it hit me.

His wife. Finkle's wife.

She left him. Twelve years ago. Moved up to the city.

Dad's voice was in my head. *Anything could have happened, I suppose.*

All of a sudden, I was wide awake.

Finkle's car — in a locked shed, drowned, with her head inside it.

Finkle's wife — gone.

I sat bolt upright and snapped on the light.

There was no way I could sleep now. This was like one of those shows on TV where the dead contact the living, unable to rest until someone uncovers the truth about their untimely death.

I had to do something.

But what could I do here, in my room, in the middle of the night?

I did the only thing I could think of.

I pulled out my box.

I leafed through the maps and the drawings and the diagrams.

How stupid had I been? That shed was nowhere near Finkle's place, nowhere near anything Finkle had anything to do with. It was out in back of the Porters' property, where no one went but the sheep. Why would Finkle abandon his clunker there unless he had something to hide?

Something big.

Sheet by sheet, I made my way through the history of Old Lower Grange, through "A Town on the Move" and "Greenies up a Tree" and "One Big Step for

Progress," through the photos of the old town and the new site and the construction work and half the town gathered up at the dam to watch Finkle flip the lever.

I don't know what I was looking for. Something. Anything.

Something that would sit at the still center of the puzzle and bring all the other pieces into an orderly orbit around it.

I sat. I read. I read some more. I stretched out my legs. I crossed them again. I got up off the floor and went to my desk, balancing the box on my bed, then reaching down into it to pull out each page in turn.

The too-many bakeries. The timber mill. The artists' studio. There was Dad in his beard, Elijah in his tree house.

I loved this stuff. But would it tell me anything? Anything apart from what it already had?

It was getting late. Early. There were no more shadows on the walls, only the early morning sun beginning to filter through.

I leaned back in my chair and stretched my arms up high, lacing my fingers together and cracking my knuckles.

I put the pages back into the box. When they were all away, I weighted them down the way I always did — with the clay mermaid I had made all those years ago.

It was packed in newspaper and Bubble Wrap to keep it safe, but that also meant you couldn't see inside. That hadn't bothered me before. I knew what it looked like. But suddenly I wanted to see it. Now that Liam and I were really diving down into the lake, not exactly like mermaids but probably as close as I would ever get, I couldn't resist the urge to open it up, to take a look at where my four-year-old artistic vision had led me.

I pulled the Bubble Wrap off, then started on the newspaper. Dad had wrapped it carefully for me in thick, cushioning layers, and now I peeled them off, one by one. Two by . . .

What?

I stared down at the paper I was holding, had been just about to toss on the floor behind me.

Dad's patented super-secure wrapping service. Old newspaper.

Old photos.

Was that *Finkle*?

I set the partially wrapped mermaid to one side and

smoothed the sheet of paper out on the desk in front of me.

It was.

It was a photo of Finkle shaking some kid's hand and presenting him with an award.

"Highest Fund-raiser," the headline read. It was some Jump Rope thing, like we did at school. This kid had raised the most money in the state, and Finkle was "delighted, absolutely delighted" to take this opportunity at the annual Lenton Festival to present him with his prize of a gift certificate and a handsome framed certificate with genuine fake-gold lettering.

And also to take him for a spin.

I don't think it was part of the official prize.

The kid was just lucky.

Because Mayor Finkle had that very day taken ownership of his pride and joy — a brand-new S-Class Mercedes — in which he was about to take Marcus Scragg, age ten, on an extremely smooth and luxurious ride.

There was a photo of it right there behind them.

It was red and shiny, so shiny it might blind you if you looked directly at it.

It most definitely was not a clunker.

I ran my fingers over the photograph.

A brand-new Mercedes.

I didn't know what S-Class meant, but the article made it sound like it was something special.

That was weird. Nobody picks up a new car, the kind of car you boast about and have your photo taken with in the paper, then ditches it in a shed without a good reason.

I unwrapped my mermaid and set it in front of me on the desk.

It didn't look much like a mermaid really. If I was truthful, it looked more like a girl who had been born with a series of unfortunate deformities. But Dad had said it was great.

He had fired it and glazed it and wrapped it carefully in soft padded layers.

It had waited in the box for me all these years to tell me something.

Something big.

Now I had to tell someone else.

Twenty-one

When I got to the fence, I froze.

The gate was wide open. There was a silver truck parked next to it.

Finkle, back already. Getting a head start on his fence-electrification research.

I looked wildly around me. There was no one in sight.

I wheeled my bike through the trees to the gap in the fence. When I got there, I froze again.

Liam's bike was there. He was here already, in the water, maybe.

Caught?

I moved quietly through the trees.

There was someone in the water, but it wasn't him.

It was Finkle, grandma-stroking around about 150 feet offshore, pausing every now and then to duck his head under the water.

Searching for something.

He wasn't in the right spot though, not quite.

And he didn't have goggles or flippers or an underwater flashlight that would last him even five seconds.

"Cassie!"

Liam was crouched behind a low bush a little way along the shoreline. His knees were grazed and bleeding.

"Did he see you?"

He shook his head. "I heard the truck. He did a massive skid when he pulled up."

I pointed at his legs. "What happened?"

He reddened. "I fell over, running for the trees. I had the flippers on."

I held back a smile at the thought. "What did you —?"

"Shh!" Liam said suddenly. "He's coming out."

Finkle waded out through the shallows.

I turned to Liam. "The car we found — it's not a clunker," I said softly.

"Yeah, I . . ." He trailed off.

Finkle had stopped and bent down toward the ground. When he straightened, he had something in his hand. He held it up, and it glinted, bright in the afternoon sun.

Liam groaned.

"What is it?" I whispered.

"I was going to show you. I dropped it when I was running."

"So what is it?"

"A hood ornament. I broke it off the car."

As we watched, Finkle closed his hand over the shape. Then he turned and headed back up toward the fence, collecting his towel and bundle of clothes from a grassy patch on the way.

We heard the clinking of metal as he pulled the gate shut and relocked it. Then we waited for the sound of the engine roaring to life and fading away down the hill before we headed out into the open.

"It's a Mercedes," Liam said. He traced the three-point logo with a stick in the dirt.

"I know."

"It could still be a clunker. Mercedes get old too."

"It's not a clunker," I repeated.

I walked over to a spreading gum tree and sat down in the shade. Liam followed me, the flippers in one hand.

"It's an S-Class," I said. "It was new."

Liam stared at me. "An S-Class? How do you even . . . how do you know that?"

I took a deep breath.

I told him about the head and the photo and the car, about Marcus Scragg.

"But why would he do that?" Liam was shaking his head. "Why would he . . . ?"

He looked out at the lake.

And this was it, I thought. This was the moment when I told him. When everything came together — all the tiny pieces of the puzzle slotting into one another perfectly, and him nodding and saying, *Oh, my God* and *Wow*.

Then what would we do? Dive down again, probably. We needed to be sure. Absolutely one hundred percent certain beyond a shadow of a doubt. We needed more evidence. And we needed to get it fast, because Finkle had the hood ornament. He knew the car was right there somewhere. He knew something was happening.

I stood up. "We have to go out," I said. "Now."

"Cassie." Liam narrowed his eyes. "What's going on?"

"It's Mrs. Finkle," I said. "I think she's in the car."

Liam exploded with laughter, sending a storm of white cockatoos fleeing from a nearby tree. "What? Are you joking?" He cocked his head to one side. "You're joking, right?"

I shook my head. "She 'left him,'" I said, making air quotes with my fingers. "She —"

Liam laughed again. "She lives in Paterson," he said. "She calls Mom all the time."

"Huh?"

"She's not *dead*, Cassie."

"Oh. But, then . . ."

"What, did you think he *killed* her? You've been watching too much TV or something. And even if he did, why would he put her in the car? Why not just put her in the shed?"

He was right. And suddenly I felt like an idiot.

All that late-night reading, the mermaid, the news-paper.

I looked past Liam, out at the water.

It still didn't make sense. There was still a car under there. Not a clunker but a new car, the kind of car you want to take some kid for a spin in and get your picture in the paper with.

Even if your wife was still alive and well and living in Paterson, why would you lock your fancy new car in someone else's shed and drown it?

Liam shrugged. "There's probably some reason."

"Yeah." Some reason. Like the invisible line across the lake saying NO SWIMMING. Swim here but not here. No need to ask questions. It's better this way.

"I don't know." I reached down beside me to pick up a gum leaf. It was one of those leaves that curls back on itself, like a dog chasing its tail, making a tiny, perfect "o" in its own center. "It doesn't make sense."

I couldn't get that picture out of my head. I had thought the newspaper was the key, that it was moving everything into place around it. Had I really imagined it?

"I don't get it," I said. "It was new at the festival, on January 16, and then —"

Beside me, I felt Liam tense, his whole body stiff, like he was bracing to ward something off.

"What?"

Liam shook his head tightly. "It doesn't matter. It's just . . . January 16, you know?"

The date. I hadn't realized at first. Why would I? It wasn't a date that mattered to me, some random day in January months before I was even born. But it meant something to lots of people. Different things. *Second Friday in January, hottest day in three years, first day of the Lenton Festival, the day I got an award and a ride in a sports car.*

The day I was a baby in the backseat of a car, my father in the front, my calm, steady brother beside me.

"Sorry," I began. "I . . ."

"It's okay. It's just a day." He reached for a leaf. "You can stop making that face now."

But I couldn't. I couldn't stop staring at him, and I couldn't stop my face from doing whatever it was doing, because all of a sudden I had no control over it. All of a sudden it took everything I had to follow the thoughts that tumbled one after the other through my head.

January 16.

HF, HF, HF.

Drawing invisible lines.

Electrifying the fence.

Keeping his name out of the minutes.

Driving his brand-new car home from Lenton on the night of the festival.

The night of the crash.

His red car, his love of speed.

My stomach lurched as I remembered how we'd had to hold on as he careered around the corners, sliding out in the gravel.

Then it lurched again, sickeningly — that last moment on the roller coaster before the bottom drops out of the world.

His red car.

My skin prickled.

"Oh, my God," I gasped.

"What?" Liam was staring at me.

I didn't know what to say, where to begin, how to

give him the piece that would click everything else into place.

"Your dad hates red," I said.

"So?"

"He hates red," I repeated. "It's his car. It's that date. He doesn't want anyone swimming here."

"There are snags and stuff," Liam countered. "He's —"

"No, there aren't," I said quietly.

I told him about the minutes. About *HF, HF, HF.*

A bubble of silence rose in the space between us.

It was Liam who broke it. "He's our friend," he said. "He's helped us out for years." He looked up at me, as if willing me to agree with him, to nod and tell him he was right. "Mom said that after the accident, there were two kinds of people. She said some of her so-called friends just disappeared. They didn't know what to say, how to handle it." He shoveled one foot in front of him through the dirt. "As if it was something *they* had to handle."

I nodded.

"But then there were other people who came out of nowhere, helping and stuff."

"Like the Finkles?"

"Yeah. Mom even said they split up around then. They had their own problems, but it didn't matter. They were always calling us, seeing how we were doing, helping out with things. Still do."

"Like with a job for your dad," I said softly, "and money for camp."

"And other stuff." Liam's words came out in a rush, falling over one another. "I mean, they've been really . . ."

He stopped.

And I saw the moment when he saw what I did, laid out before him, the moment the last piece dropped into the pit of his stomach, like a small, cold stone.

"The license plates are gone," he said slowly. "I thought it was because it was a clunker."

"What should we do?"

"I don't know. Something." He looked away quickly, blinking.

"We need proof," I said. Proof that the car was even under there, for a start.

And maybe more.

"Maybe there'll be something there," I said. "Some-

190

thing like . . ." I trailed off. Because I didn't know how to say the words that would bring that fiery picture to life for both of us — words like *scratch* or *dent*. *Something that proved he was there,* I wanted to say, *in his car, going too fast, causing "Local Man/Horror Smash," something that had nothing at all to do with "fatigue" or "driver error" — or a crying baby.*

I didn't need to say it. Liam turned back to me, his jaw set hard.

"I'm going out again."

"I'll get the raft."

I wouldn't time him today, wouldn't count *one-cat-and-dog* or watch the surface for bubbles.

I would just wait. I knew he would stay down as long as he needed to. As long as he could.

"Cassie, stop!"

Liam grabbed my arm and pulled me down into the shade of the tree.

There was a crunch of tires, a rattling of chains.

We edged our way back into the scrub, keeping low.

It was Finkle again, changed back into his clothes but still slightly damp-looking. There were two other men with him. They were nodding as Finkle pointed out across the water and then down at the edge.

Liam gripped my arm. "What's he doing?"

"I don't know, but I don't think we can swim here today."

The men were unpacking tripods and cameras and collapsible rulers from a case. One of them was punching buttons on some kind of handheld electronic device.

It looked like they were settling in.

"Tomorrow," Liam said. "During the centenary."

Yes. It was perfect. We could show our faces for a while, then slip away. There was no way Finkle could be here then. Not when he had a lever to flip and a head to unveil and a time capsule to bury.

We crouched low and crept along the tree line toward our bikes.

I glanced down at Liam's leg. Blood was flowing from the graze on his knee. "You should clean that," I said. "It could get infected."

Liam shook his head as he slipped ahead of me through the break in the fence. "Don't worry about me," he said. "I'm going to be fine."

Twenty-two

Hannah made me wear my best clothes.

"Howard will want you in a photo," she said.

I tucked my shirt into my pants, then did up an extra button near the collar so you couldn't see my bathing suit underneath.

It wasn't my normal swimsuit. My Speedo was tumbling around and around in the washing machine, soaked in water and detergent.

"All that chlorine," Mom said. "It's good to give it a proper wash every now and then. And it's not like you'll be needing it today, is it?"

I shook my head. Then I went and grabbed the stripy bikini from the drawer where I had stuffed it.

It felt wrong, like I was wearing nothing at all. The flimsy straps sat there loosely rather than snapping securely across my back.

It wouldn't matter today. It wasn't like I was going to be doing my six or anything. And I could leave my shirt over the top for diving.

The ceremony was at one. The grand unveiling of the Finkle head and the mosaic and the hand-prints, the flipping of the new fake lever, the burying of the time capsule, the off-key blaring of the brass band.

Then some photos, some potato salad, maybe a ceremonial sausage or two.

But by then, Liam and I would be long gone.

We'd be up at the lake with the underwater camera he had borrowed from his mother's cousin's second-best friend. It had a built-in flash that was way better than a leaky flashlight.

We would get evidence. We would piece the puzzle together carefully and exactly so no one could take it apart.

We gathered near the clock tower — the class, the

community, everyone in New Lower Grange, and plenty of other people besides.

Hannah was beaming. There were journalists from the city with notebooks and clipboards. There was even a TV crew with microphones and cameras.

Hannah walked around, shaking hands and welcoming everyone.

On a trestle table nearby, copies of the centenary book were stacked in neat, tidy rows.

I stood in my best clothes, buttoned up one hole too high, and waited.

Then Hannah's phone rang, and I saw her frown. She shook her head. She opened her mouth, said a few words, closed it again. Then she hung up and looked around with a panicked expression at the gathering crowd.

It was 12:45.

She walked to the podium and tapped the microphone. "Ladies and gentlemen," she began, "I do apologize. There may be a slight delay. The mayor has some urgent business to attend to. Rest assured he will be with us as soon as possible."

A slight delay? How slight was slight? I wondered. And what was urgent business, anyway? Was this more Finkle-spin, and we'd be standing here all afternoon while he trimmed his beard?

I grabbed Hannah before she could disappear into the crowd. "What's going on?"

"Howard had to go to check on the water guys."

"What water guys?"

She waved a hand. "Oh, they're letting more water into the lake or something."

"They're what?" My heart raced. "But what for?"

"Howard says it's too low," Hannah said. "It's getting dangerous for boating and stuff. Lots of snags or something." She sighed. "If I'd known about it, we could have had the ceremony up there. It would have been symbolic. But it was all a bit last minute — too late to move things." She checked her watch and frowned. "I hope he won't be long."

"Finkle's flipping a lever?"

"What?" She shook her head. "There's no lever."

"But he's drowning the town, right — all over again?"

"Cassie, do you have to be so dramatic? It's just a bit

of extra water. It's not the same thing at all." Then she leaned toward me. "Aren't you hot like that? Why don't you undo . . ."

I took a step back, out of reach. Then another. Then I turned and hurried through the crowd, searching for Liam.

Finkle was going to drown the town, the car, everything all over again.

It would be sunk deep, so deep we would never get back down there. The water rushing in would break up the car, tumble it over itself, send its rusted pieces flying in all directions.

And we had no proof, just a pile of wood and a mirror that could be from anywhere.

No one would believe us.

I wouldn't believe us, if I wasn't already me.

I raced through the crowd and finally spotted Liam over by the headless plinth. He was wearing dark trousers, but underneath I could see the telltale lines of his board shorts.

"We have to go!" he said when I told him. "We have to go now."

I nodded. But how? There was no time. No time to

go back for our bikes and ride up there. There was no time at all.

We stared at each other hopelessly.

There was no way.

Then I heard a familiar noise. An engine chugging and spluttering as it pulled into the parking lot: old, worn brakes squealing in protest.

A faded, rusty, once-green truck held together by duct tape and optimism.

I grabbed Liam by the wrist. "Let's go."

Twenty-three

"You're kidding!" Elijah said. "You've got to be kidding!"

"Not kidding," I said.

Next to me, Liam shook his head, tight-lipped.

It was squashy in the front seat of the truck. I was jammed up sideways against the door with the handle sticking into my side.

We were getting there, though. We were getting there fast.

Elijah hadn't even argued.

When we ran toward him babbling, *Finkle* and *lever* and *hurry!,* he just nodded and said, "Get in." Then he threw the truck into reverse and squealed out of the parking lot.

On the way, we explained. That is, I explained and Liam's hands clenched slowly into fists on his lap.

"Wow," Elijah said. "Seriously? Are you sure?"

I glanced at Liam. Were we? Was I? I had felt sure before about Mrs. Finkle, and it turned out I had known exactly nothing.

"Yeah," I said. "I mean, I think so."

"Unbelievable." Elijah flattened his foot on the accelerator.

When we turned off the highway, my heart sank. The barrier across the dirt road was locked in place.

But Elijah didn't even blink. He slowed only slightly, then veered around the barrier, through the long grass and onto the rough road.

It was a bumpier ride than the one we'd done with Finkle. Elijah's truck wasn't really up to this kind of driving any more. It wasn't up to much of anything.

We struggled and strained up the hill and around the bends, Elijah easing his foot on and off the accelerator, leaning forward, a look of determination on his face.

Finally, we skidded around the last bend, pulling up

in front of the fence, with its gate and its warning signs and its chunky, padlocked chain.

Padlocked. Not open.

There were no cars here. No official-looking men. There was no one.

I jumped out of the truck and ran for the break in the fence, sprinting through the tree line and down to the water's edge.

There was nothing and no one, and for a minute I couldn't work it out — why Hannah had said that, where Finkle had gone.

And then I looked up. And out. Across the water to the dam wall, which curved up high in the distance.

Of course. Of course, they weren't here. They were where the controls were, all the way up at the power station, probably. Finkle and the engineers and the computers, deciding where the water went and when it went there.

Meaning here. Meaning now.

But then something moved on the dam wall. There was a figure, a small shape in the distance, silhouetted against the sun.

There was someone there.

And that was closer. Close enough?

"We have to go around," Liam said, coming up behind me.

"There's no time."

Even though it was closer than the power station, it was still too far — all the way back down to the road, all the way around on the highway, the long, stupid distance to a swimming hole that was so far away it never made sense to anyone but Finkle.

We could run around the edge of the lake — through the trees and the scrub, past the Point and the viewing platform, and all the way along the wall. But that was a long way, too. Too long.

What we needed was a straight line from here to there.

I looked out across the lake.

"The raft!" Liam darted across the open ground toward the bush we kept it hidden behind.

But I shook my head.

The raft was too slow. It was heavy. It zigged and zagged.

I was stronger these days. I was faster.

I ran to the water's edge. I kicked my shoes off and dived in.

Just before I hit the water, I heard Elijah yelling behind me.

"Cassie! Don't —"

It's an odd thing when you're swimming. You can't hear anything much. It's like watching a video clip with the sound off, seeing everyone screaming at you from the sidelines as you turn to take a breath.

If I was too slow, I thought, if they flipped the lever and the water came at me, first in a trickle, spilling down the wall, then in a raging torrent, hopefully I wouldn't hear that, either.

I knew I wouldn't see it. I was breathing only on the right, not turning my head toward the wall. There was no time for Mr. Henshall today. All of that stuff about rules and technique and following the black line up and down, up and down, felt like it was a million years ago.

Today it was all about speed.

I should probably have thought of that before

I dived in with my clothes on. My pants were heavy around my legs, and my shirtsleeves flapped with every stroke I took.

I couldn't stop now, though. I had to keep going, to keep my head down and just get there.

Out into the middle, past the drowned car and the fire tree and the pointless NO SWIMMING sign.

Farther. Faster.

How long would it take? Fifteen minutes? Twenty?

It was hard to predict distance across the open water.

I lifted my head for a second, making sure I was still lined up with the edge of the wall. When I got there, I'd haul myself out. I'd run up the little stairs etched into the side of the slope, all the way to the top.

I'd tell whoever was up there everything — about Finkle and the car and the red and . . . just everything.

I looked over at the stairs. Swim there, climb the stairs, run along the top of the wall.

I had come the quickest way, but it was still too long.

There was no time.

I turned back toward the wall. Maybe ten pool lengths away. Fifteen hundred feet.

I couldn't have swum it a few months ago, not after making it this far already.

Fifteen hundred feet. Less than ten minutes.

And I didn't need to swim it all. I didn't need to get right up against the dam wall. Just close enough. Close enough to be seen and heard.

Close enough that I would be in the way.

I reached down and pulled my socks off, then my pants, leaving them floating on the surface of the water in my wake.

Then I set off toward the wall, alternating strokes — swimming freestyle for speed, then the grandma stroke so I could see.

About 150 feet back from the wall, I stopped. I took my shirt off. I peeled it off and held it above my head, waving it around and around.

"Hey!" I yelled at the top of my lungs. "Hey!"

The figure turned. Even from this distance, I could tell it was the round shape of Finkle.

There was no one else there, but he was waving one arm and yelling. No, not yelling. Just talking loudly. Into the phone he had pressed to one ear.

The phone that connected him to the power station,

to the engineers and the computers.

Did he see me? I didn't know. I only knew that as I watched and yelled and waved my shirt, he turned back toward the river and motioned with one arm, sweeping it down toward the ground in a strong, swift movement like someone dropping the flag for the start of a race.

There was a sound, low and heavy, like something shifting. Then another underneath it, or over the top, maybe. They were mixed up together, so I couldn't separate one from the other. I looked around me to see where it was coming from, what was happening.

And I saw it — slow at first, a trickle. Then faster, steadier.

Water starting to gush out from the dam wall.

Water that had churned and boiled over itself through the massive pipes, rushing at the press of a button all the way down the mountain, all the way here, to the wall, to the lake.

To me.

Then I heard something else.

A horn blaring, over and over, back from the other side of the lake. An old green truck bumping and rattling its way around the edges, broken pieces of wire mesh dragging from its hood.

Liam was leaning out the passenger-side window, pointing and waving his arms wildly toward me.

Water was spilling down the walls, faster now and harder. I shot a glance to the side, toward the bank. Could I swim for it? I didn't see how. To get to the steps, to get anywhere I'd be able to scramble up for higher ground, I would have to head in toward the wall, where the water was churning.

I looked behind me, toward the fire tree. Maybe I could make it there, stay ahead of the water? I could hang on to the stick, on to the tree, while the lake rose up toward me, and maybe, just maybe, I would be high enough.

A mechanical sound buzzed in the air, and the water around me whipped up suddenly. *It's coming!*, I thought. *It's too late.* I braced myself to hang on, to hold my breath for as long as I could, willing myself not to count so I wouldn't have to notice the exact moment I ran out of air.

But then the sound grew louder and the water fanned out strangely around me, and I realized it wasn't coming from the wall. And when I looked up, there was a helicopter with GTV-NEWS on the side and a man hanging out the door with a camera, waving.

Around me, the water whipped up like the middle of the choppy ocean, but when I could see a path through the spray, I saw that the flow down the dam wall had eased. And as I watched, it slowed and slowed until it came to a stop.

And even from here, even through the spray and the fog of my raggedy breathing and my still-waving shirt, I saw Finkle's arm drop, the phone falling silent by his side. Then his shoulders slumped, like someone straggling across the line, defeated, at the end of a race.

Twenty-four

They didn't drown the town.

Instead, two days later, they sent down a diver. He had flippers and a face mask and a proper underwater flashlight. And an oxygen tank, so he didn't have to count and gasp and rocket himself off the bottom.

After a while, he came up. He frog-walked over to talk to the police sergeant, who frowned and nodded, then called to some other men who were waiting on the bank with a truck and a winch and some long metal cables.

Then the diver went back down, hauling the chains under with him, and slowly, carefully, they dragged the car up into the light.

I didn't know how to feel. On the one hand, it was a relief that there was no Mrs. Finkle down there. That there would be no trunk popping open to reveal a skeleton, no bony arm lolling from a window.

But it felt wrong to be relieved. Because there was a body. Just not here. And I couldn't help thinking about Liam's brother — about Luke — just down the hall from me in the hospital.

I wasn't there — not really — but I could remember it all the same.

The whole town gathered to watch the car come up. They came quietly up the hill, without potato salad or sausages.

The sign said AUTHORIZED PERSONNEL ONLY, but no one cared. They swung the busted gates open wide and pushed on through.

Liam sat with his mother and father on the edge of the bank and waited. All around, people were craning and leaning forward for the first glimpse, but no one moved in front of them.

Out on the lake, chains clanked and the old metal groaned. As the car broke the surface, tiny creatures scuttled across the hood and jumped for their lives. Water streamed down the sides, and lake weed hung from every angle, strung across the panels like raggedy stitches.

Liam's dad stood up.

The car wasn't the flashy bright red of a Mercedes anymore, but it was still red.

The whole town turned toward him.

He watched it hanging from the crane, swinging there like a pendulum, with the long dark wound in its side, the scrape of blue paint they would test later and discover exactly matched the paint on the Prices' old car.

And he pumped his fist into the air and smiled.

Finkle confessed. As soon as the car came up, as soon as people saw the great smashed dent in its side, he started talking.

It was late. He was tired. It was a steep hill. He may have been going too fast. Oh, but it was hard to remember; it was such a very long time ago.

Wait, yes. No, it wasn't. He had been going too fast. Much too fast.

He hadn't stopped.

At the stop sign. Or afterward.

He had plowed into the Prices' car, sending it spinning and spinning toward the clock tower.

He had spun and spun, too, then found himself straight, back on the road. Panicking. Driving away.

There was no excuse for it. No excuse at all.

He talked on and on. He put his head in his hands. Journalists tried to ask him questions, but they couldn't get a word in. It was like he had been waiting to let this out all these years. It was like a dam bursting.

He was famous now, just as he'd always hoped. Except instead of "Centenary Mayor" and "Landmark Event," it was "Local Mayor Admits Hit-and-Run" and "Mystery Car at Bottom of Lake."

And my personal favorite: "Unlikely Atlantis Reveals Its Secrets."

They put me in the paper, too: "Local Girl Swims Lake: Brave Dash Uncovers Truth."

I had made those stories.

And some others.

Already Elijah was saying, *You looked so tiny all the way out there* and *Mate, my brain just went blank*; and

Hannah was saying, *That was so sneaky, the way you had your shirt all buttoned up — I knew something was going on*; and Mom was saying, *I can't believe you went up there all on your own* and *I almost died when I saw it on the news.*

They played the footage over and over — of me in the lake in my striped bikini, waving my shirt, of Finkle bringing his arm down, of Liam leaning out the window of the car, pointing, like a soldier leading a charge.

When I thanked Elijah for sounding his horn, he grinned. "I had to do something, you idiot."

But when I thanked him for calling the TV crew, he shook his head. "That wasn't me," he said. "That was Hannah."

"Hannah?"

He nodded. "I called her, but my battery was running down. My brain was, too. I didn't know what to do. I just yelled at her about Finkle and the car and you in the lake, and she went all quiet for a second, then said, *Right, leave it to me,* and the next thing I knew . . ."

The helicopter. It came so quickly, so dramatically.

It was in the way, just like I was. It was impossible to ignore.

That was one thing about Hannah. She had always been good at doing what needed to be done.

The helicopter hovered over me, and someone threw down a rope. I grabbed on, and they towed me to the bank on the opposite side.

I was right in the end.

It really wasn't that far.

Twenty-five

"Are you ready?"

Liam nodded.

We were flat on our stomachs, hanging off the raft. Not out by the fire tree, not over the town. Just out in the middle of the lake, in the middle of nowhere.

I let it go.

The head bobbed for a second, hanging in the water as if it was making up its mind, as if it had a choice in the matter.

Then it sank. Down and down, away from the raft, away from the light.

I knew what that felt like, but I wasn't going to reach out for it, wasn't going to extend a stick, or a hand, to haul it back up.

I lay alongside Liam, and we didn't speak, didn't blink.

We watched Finkle disappear.

The Finkle head, which had sat on its plinth for less than a day before Hannah took it down. Which had sat in Dad's studio for less than an hour while he said he didn't know what to do with it, that he didn't even want it for his creepy zombie garden. Which had sat in my backpack and then between us on the raft and was now sinking, down into the lake.

And I mustn't have dropped it quite straight. I must have put a little twist on it accidentally as I let it go, because as we watched, it slowly began to rotate, spiraling its way downward and out of sight.

I looked over at Liam and grinned.

It was doing the Finkle-spin.

Out on the water, people were swimming and diving and paddling in the shadows. There were kids on rubber rings and inflatable horses. There were parents on the bank with ice chests and folding chairs.

Over at the fire tree, Amber was hauling herself down the pegs while Emily floated nearby on a hot-pink air mattress.

And coming toward us across the lake was Liam's dad — not zigging or zagging or lifting his head to correct his course but just swimming straight for the raft in long, easy strokes.

"Your dad's a good swimmer," I said to Liam.

"Who do you think taught me?"

His father slowed as he neared the raft, and I inched sideways so he had space to hold on.

He would want to rest when he got here, to take a break. Even though he made it look easy, I knew he was working hard out there, invisibly, underwater.

Swimming was about staying on the surface, but sometimes to stay afloat, to keep moving, you had to figure out what was going on underneath.

Sometimes you had to dig deeper, dive down for things.

I stood up. "Coming in?"

Liam grinned.

We flattened our feet to the rough wood, pushing down for the surest footing we could find on a raft, in the middle of a lake, suspended over a drowned town.

We coiled like springs, waiting.

Then we launched ourselves — out into the sunlight.

We sliced the water like butter, knifing down and down into the cool and the dark and the cold and the vast underneath.

Above us, I heard Liam's father laughing and laughing.

It turned out you could break through the smooth surface of anything if you just kept pushing hard enough.